Surrendering

SWANS LANDING #4

SHANA NORRIS

My soul is full of longing
for the secret of the sea.

- Henry Wadsworth Longfellow

Chapter 1

The world had turned into an endless stretch of gray. Gray water, gray clouds, gray sky.

How could I be sure we were swimming in the right direction when all I could see was gray everywhere? There was nothing to indicate which direction was which, or that the place we'd been hoping to see for the last month and a half was almost within reach.

When I stopped swimming to examine the horizon, my half-sister Sailor Mooring swam to my side. Even she looked gray. The circles that had appeared under her eyes after our last swim across the Atlantic had deepened even more during this second swim. She had always been thin, but now cheekbones looked on the verge of poking through her skin and the water lapped at her shoulder just below her sharp collarbone.

My gaze switched to the woman at Sailor's side. Coral Mooring, her mother, had the same gray emaciated look. But Coral had looked that way even when we'd found her back in Hether Blether, one of the vanishing islands of our people.

No, I reminded myself. The finfolk in Hether Blether were not *our* people. Our people had left the homeland centuries ago in search of a different life. We had almost nothing in common with the savage finfolk that still lived there under the rule of Domnall, the finfolk king.

"What is it?" Callum Murchadh asked in his thick Scottish brogue. Wet red hair clung to his pale face as he studied me. Callum was perceptive and I should have known that he would notice my hesitation.

I shook my head. "Nothing. I must be mistaken."

"What's wrong, Josh?" Sailor asked, a tight edge to her voice.

I scanned the area around us again, searching through the mist that hung over the water for the dark shape I hoped to see. *Needed* to see.

But it wasn't there. I had paid close attention to the path Sailor and I had taken from our home of Swans Landing when we'd first left back in March. I took note of the landmarks that would tell us where we were and estimated the swimming distance between each one in my head. I had a good memory. I didn't think I'd forgotten anything, especially not something this important. I remembered everything, from the earliest memory I had at age three—I'd spelled "Joshua Oliver Canavan" with my wooden blocks—to the scent of Mara Westray's body wash that I hadn't smelled in five months. My memory was great.

But something else wasn't right.

We had passed the black and white striped lighthouse of Cape Hatteras. Then the short white lighthouse of Ocracoke. The next one should have been the white lighthouse with the single black stripe that stood on the northern end of Swans Landing.

Only it hadn't yet appeared.

Maybe I was wrong. Maybe I had miscalculated, or gotten my estimates mixed up.

Why couldn't I find the island where I'd lived my entire life?

"It should be here," I said to the others, unable to meet their gaze as they watched me.

"What should?" Sailor asked. Her eyes were wide and she looked like she was on the verge of breaking down. She was known for her epic tantrums, but she had been through a lot in the last five months and this second swim across thousands of miles of ocean was probably wearing her down.

"The island," I said softly.

"What do you mean?" Callum asked, stopping Sailor before she could speak again. He stayed close to her, as he had done for most of the swim. Sometimes he fell behind because he didn't have a full tail like the rest of us. In his human form, his right leg had been cut off just above the knee. In his finfolk form, half of his tail ended in scarred edges. "Where is the island?"

I shook my head. "I don't know. I remember all the places we saw along the way when we first left. I kept track of the lighthouses, because they were the easiest landmarks to spot from the water. I counted them as we swam and estimated the distance between each one. We should have passed Swans Landing already."

Callum and Sailor stared at me, neither one speaking as the words hung in the air like the mists over the water. A bird cawed somewhere above our heads, lost in the clouds. Coral didn't look too worried. She only hummed softly to herself, the sound barely audible.

"You must be wrong," Sailor said finally. "We're not there yet."

"Maybe we passed too far out to see the light," I said. But the light from the Swans Landing Lighthouse was meant to be seen far out in the water, which was known as the Graveyard of the Atlantic. The lighthouses provided a warning for ships and we should have been close enough to the islands to easily see the light.

Except that the fog hanging over the water was as thick as a woolen blanket. It was hard to see even more than a few feet away.

"Let's swim back the way we came," Callum said. He grimaced as he spoke, and I knew swimming for so long wasn't easy for him with his damaged tail. But he hadn't complained at all and had kept up as best he could. There was no other choice. If he had fallen behind or if we had slowed down for him, it would give Domnall and the other finfolk the chance to catch up.

We had to reach Swans Landing before they did. We had to warn everyone what was coming.

"Let's keep swimming," I agreed.

I estimated the distance we swam in my head as we headed back in the other direction. If we went too far, we'd end up in Ocracoke, the island just north of Swans Landing. Our home was the most remote of the inhabited islands along the Outer Banks, accessible only by a ferry that ran between the island and the mainland three times a day.

Unless you happened to be finfolk, of course. Then the ferry schedule didn't have much hold over you.

I reached for the heavy iron bar that I had tucked into the belt of my wet robe. It looked like an ordinary twisted piece of metal, but it was much more than that. It was the key that had led us to Hether Blether on the other side of the ocean. It had guided us when we most needed help.

We need help now, I thought as I gripped the key in my fist. The key was tied to the finfolk lands, but I didn't know if Swans Landing counted. It was inhabited by both finfolk and humans, and had never had a tie to the finfolk homeland like Hether Blether did.

But at the moment, we needed all the help we could get.

As we swam, I let my mind wander and think about home. Sitting on the beach at Pirate's Cove. My mom, smiling and happy when she had one of her good days. Playing my guitar

4

in front of Moody's Variety Store on Friday nights. The sound of the finfolk singing from the water on Song Night.

The warmth of Mara Westray in my arms.

I ached for home so badly that I could see it in front of me, the little village rising from the mists like a mirage. The clang of the morning ferry as it got ready to depart the island echoed over the water.

"There it is!" Sailor exclaimed.

I blinked, focusing on the shape in the mists ahead of me. Where there had been only gray sky a moment ago, now recognizable forms appeared solid and real. The lighthouse blinked across the water, over the tops of the trees and houses that surrounded it.

I couldn't help letting out a whoop before I dove under the water, swimming as hard as I could toward the island. I flicked my tail, sending up an explosion of bubbles all around me. I twisted and turned, bucking and diving under the water as elation spread through me.

We were home. We had made it. We had beat Domnall. Everything would be all right now.

I surfaced again to stare into the distance, sure that when I looked again the island would be gone. But there it was still, waiting for us to reach it, the pull of the earth becoming stronger inside me, calling me home—

"Josh!" Sailor's shout pierced the air, tearing my gaze away from the island ahead of me. I spun around in the water to look at her.

But Sailor wasn't looking at me. She stared at something to my left, her eyes wide and her face paler than before.

I turned just in time to see the gray tip of a fin slice through the water before it disappeared under the surface. Before I had a chance to even blink, the searing pain of teeth piercing my arm exploded through my body.

Chapter 2

Teeth ground into my bones as I struggled to get free, letting out a strangled cry. As I flailed, hitting the shark with the finfolk key still clutched in my other hand, I could see that it wasn't a large shark, but it was large enough. It certainly had teeth big enough to do damage.

Callum swam to my side, grabbing my other arm with one hand and then beating at the shark's nose with his free hand. The shark bit down harder, thrashing in the blood-stained water. All the time that I had swam in my life, I had never worried about being mistaken for food by another sea creature. Maybe it was the human part of me that still thought of myself as separate from the rest of the ocean life, but I knew now that I was wrong. Here in the ocean, I wasn't the fastest or strongest creature, maybe not even the smartest. In the cycle of life under the water, I was just another prospective meal for any number of creatures.

My superiority had come to an end as the shark's teeth bit deeper into muscle and bone.

Callum drew back his hand and punched the shark hard in the side of its head. The world spun as a wave of dizziness washed over me.

Callum's punch must have stunned the shark just enough that it let go. Callum snatched me back, pulling me behind him as he struggled to swim toward shore. Sailor and her mother were already ahead of us.

Red rivers flowed behind us as Callum pulled me toward the island. I glanced down at my arm, then squeezed my eyes shut when nausea washed over me. I needed to swim, but my body was slow to respond to my commands. Gashes ran down my upper arm, open to reveal red muscle underneath. It was bad, I could tell that much just from the quick glance I'd had.

"Can you change form?" Callum grunted when we were close to land.

Dizziness washed over me again. Surprisingly, my arm didn't hurt so much anymore. But that was a bad thing, wasn't it? I tried to remember everything I'd learned about injuries in health class. Shock. I should be worried about going into shock. My vision blurred for a moment and I blinked, trying to find something to focus on.

"Josh?" Callum's face appeared in front of me. "Josh, listen to me. You'll be all right, aye okay? Just follow me."

I nodded and tried to swim, but my tail didn't work right. It felt detached from the rest of me.

Sailor swam out toward us, leaving her mother closer to the shore. "Is he okay?" she asked.

"I think he's going into shock," Callum told her. "He's badly hurt."

Their voices sounded far away and the world darkened for a moment. I floated on the water, my body suddenly feeling much colder, like ice had been dumped on top of me.

Sailor grabbed my arm and looked at it, swallowing hard. "We need to sing for him."

"No," I said as another wave of dizziness washed over me. "You're too tired. Get a doctor." There was just one clinic on Swans Landing, near the northern end of the island.

"You could bleed to death before we get back with a doctor!" Sailor shouted. "I've done this before. Shut up and listen."

I tried to protest, but I slipped under the water, my mouth filling with the salty liquid. Callum's grip on my arm tightened as he pulled me back above the surface.

I tried to focus on the song Sailor started to hum, but I was tired. My eyelids felt like lead. *We should get out of the water,* I thought. The shark could come back and we were surrounded by blood. But I was too tired to say this.

Callum's voice joined Sailor's and I lay back, stretching my injured arm out to the side. It didn't hurt at all anymore. It felt warm and tingly. I was aware of an ache in my tail and heard bones popping, but even that didn't hurt.

After a moment, I felt awake and renewed. Energy I hadn't felt in months coursed through me, warming my skin and bones.

I opened my eyes, peering up at the gray sky overhead. It was summer, I remembered. My eighteenth birthday had passed—what, a week ago? Two weeks? I didn't know exactly what date it was, only that it had to be early August by now.

But why was it so cold? Where was the sun?

Sailor's face appeared in my line of vision, her dark hair hanging around her face in wet strings as she looked down at me. "You okay?" she asked, panting as she spoke.

I nodded. "I think so."

She smiled, but the smile didn't reach her eyes, which seemed dull and almost lifeless. "Good."

Then she closed her eyes and collapsed against me.

"Sailor!" She moaned softly when I shook her, but didn't open her eyes.

"It was too much for her," Callum said. He looked just as weak and tired as Sailor did. "The song takes too much energy and she was already too tired."

"Will she be okay?" I asked.

Callum nodded. "She needs rest." His jaw twitched as he swallowed. "We all do."

I felt my toes brush sand under the water. *Toes!* I had feet again. I had legs and a human body. It had been too long since I'd touched land. I could see the same ache for land that coursed through me echoed in Callum's eyes. Finfolk were never fully happy on land or water. We always wanted both.

Coral stood on the shore, holding her hair back from her face as she watched us. Her wet robe whipped around her knees in tattered edges. I recognized the little strip of beach where she stood, and the dark trees that bordered it. Pirate's Cove, the hideaway near the southern end of the island, where the sound met the ocean. The water around us swirled and foamed, crashing against the shore in a frothy mass like I had never seen before.

I slipped my arms under Sailor's body and held her against my chest. She was already changing back to human form, red scales slipping under her skin. Her head lolled against my shoulder, her eyes closed.

I nodded to Callum, who put a hand on my shoulder to steady himself for the change back to his one-legged human form. Then we made our way toward the island.

* * *

Sailor moaned a little as I gently lowered her limp body to the cold sand. Her lips chattered slightly as the wind whipped over the water toward us. Her mother sat nearby, drawing circles in the sand and humming to herself still. Coral hadn't had more than a few brief moments of clarity during our swim from Hether Blether. Sailor had hoped that bringing her home would help whatever happened to her mind, but it didn't look as though that was the case so far.

Callum flopped down onto the sand next to Sailor, panting heavily. He had his wooden prosthetic slung over his shoulder by the cloth strap, but he didn't move to put it on.

"Someone should get help," Callum said, after checking to make sure Sailor was okay.

"You mean me," I said.

He looked up, wiping wet hair away from his eyes. "You are the only one here with two working legs and a sound mind." He tossed his prosthetic into the sand. "That bloody thing hurts. I'm sure Domnall had the woodcarver make it painful on purpose."

I glanced at Coral, who was still preoccupied with her drawings. "Can you keep an eye on both of them?"

"Neither look like they're going anywhere," Callum said.

He was right. Sailor was in no condition to move, and Coral didn't seem like she would go too far at the moment.

"I'll be back as soon as I can." I scanned the water behind us, searching for anyone else emerging from the fog. But it was empty, except for the white capped waves that rolled toward shore.

"We have some time before they catch up," Callum said, sensing my hesitation. "A few days, if we're lucky."

"And if we're not?" I asked.

Callum pressed his lips together, but didn't answer.

I took a deep breath, casting another look at Sailor, then I dashed into the trees, following the familiar path through the woods. We didn't have time for second guesses. The trees of the maritime forest reached out long, spindly limbs and scratched at my face. I pushed through them, urging myself to run faster. I wished I had my ATV. I was so used to speeding across the island on it whenever I wanted to go somewhere. My legs couldn't carry me fast enough.

The streets of Swans Landing were empty. No one walked along the sidewalks, no one shopped in the few stores still open along Heron Avenue. The island looked like it did during the off-season, when cold, gray winter days kept people inside and tourists away.

Except that it was August. The summer sun should have been beating down on the sidewalk. Kids should have been outside, eating ice cream and enjoying summer vacation. Tourists should have been strolling along the sidewalks, carrying shopping bags or fishing poles.

A shiver crept up my spine and tickled across my scalp. The island looked like a ghost town. Where were the people?

My feet led me down a short, narrow street off the main road. I dashed past houses and leaped over bushes. The robe I'd been given by the finfolk king whipped around my legs as I moved.

I stumbled up the staircase to the small A-frame house and pounded on the door with my fist, not even pausing to catch my breath.

A moment later, the door whipped open and I froze as all thoughts vanished from my mind. Mara's golden brown eyes widened, her mouth open in an O shape.

"Josh?" she whispered.

I had dreamed about her every night for the last five months. Everything I had been through in the months since I'd last seen her slipped away as I stared into her eyes.

"Mara," I said, choking back the lump in my throat. I stepped forward, wrapping my arms around her and pressing her body as close to mine as I could. She still smelled the same, like salt and the lilac body wash she used to remind her of her mother.

Her lips found mine and I kissed her long and hard until my lungs felt like they'd burst.

"When did you get here?" Mara asked when she pulled away from me. She looked me up and down, her eyes roaming over my clothes and shivering shoulders. "You're soaked. Come inside and warm up." Then her gaze fell on the bloodstains on the tattered shoulder of my robe. "Oh my god. What happened? Are you okay?"

Reality crashed back into me. "Sailor," I said. "I need help with Sailor. We have to get Miss Gale—"

Mara grabbed my arm as I started to turn. "Miss Gale is sick," she told me.

I shook my head. "Miss Gale doesn't get sick." Sailor's grandmother was one of the healthiest people I had ever known. She was always seen walking around the island or raking oysters in the sound. She was still strong and solid, even as she had gotten older.

Mara's face was grim. "Apparently she does. She's been sick since you guys left. What's wrong with Sailor?" She was already stepping out the door, pulling it closed behind her.

"Is your dad home?" I asked.

"No, he's fishing," Mara said. "Josh, what's wrong?"

I swallowed, shivering again as the cold breeze hit me. "Something really bad is about to come here."

Chapter 3

Mara was the one who thought to stop at Dylan's house on the way back to Pirate's Cove. He followed without any questions as soon as he spotted me.

I pushed through the low hanging branches along the path once again, holding them up high enough for Mara to pass underneath. It was dark inside the forest, even though it was the middle of the afternoon. The sun barely broke through the gray clouds outside and almost no light filtered through the spindly branches over our heads.

"Sailor healed me," I explained. "We learned that finfolk can combine the songs of earth and water into one and use it to heal each other as we change forms."

"*Combine* them?" Dylan asked behind me, his voice loud in the silent woods. Not even birds sang from the trees around us, as if they had all disappeared. "I've never heard of anyone combining the songs. No one even sings the earth songs at all."

"There's a lot we've forgotten how to do," I told him.

"So what happened?" Mara prompted. "What's wrong with Sailor?"

"She passed out," I said. "It takes a lot of energy to use the songs like that. We did it once before, back in Hether Blether. Trust me, it's not something you want to do every day. But the shark had bitten my arm pretty deep, and Sailor stopped me from bleeding to death. We've been swimming for so long with barely any food or rest. She was too exhausted and shouldn't have tried."

"So you just let her do it and hurt herself instead?" Dylan roared. Mara and I stopped to look back at him, but he shot us a glare and then pushed past us. He ran down the path, jumping over roots and brush. We had to run to keep up.

Dylan skidded to a stop when we broke through the trees and reached the little strip of beach. Sailor still lay on the sand, her head in Callum's lap. He had reattached his prosthetic, and the wooden leg was stretched out in front of him. Coral walked along the edge of the water, picking up seashells.

Dylan's hesitation only lasted a second and then he hurried across the sand, kneeling at Sailor's side. He picked up her hand and leaned over her, his long blonde hair falling over his shoulders.

"Sailor?" he asked.

Sailor's eyes fluttered open and she smiled. "Hey," she croaked. "Bet you thought you'd never see me again, huh?"

Dylan smirked. "I knew you couldn't stay gone for good. How are you feeling? Are you hurt?"

Sailor closed her eyes, but she shook her head.

"She's tired," Callum said. "She needs to sleep for a while. And she needs food."

Dylan's gaze darted up to meet Callum's and he scowled. "Who are you?" he snapped.

"This is Callum," I explained. "We met him in Scotland. He's finfolk, and he helped us find Hether Blether." I gestured to the others. "This is Dylan and Mara."

Callum nodded and offered Dylan his hand, but Dylan ignored him and focused on Sailor. Mara stepped forward and shook Callum's hand, shooting Dylan a scowl that he didn't see.

"Oliver, look what I found." Coral rushed over to me, holding up a pearly pink seashell. Her eyes sparkled when she smiled. "Isn't it pretty?"

Mara studied Coral for a moment, then gave me a confused look. "Oliver?" she asked.

"My father," I explained. I took the shell Coral offered me and smiled gently at her. "This is Coral Mooring, Sailor's mother. We found her in Hether Blether, but she's not…not well. Something is wrong with her mind. She thinks I'm my dad sometimes and she doesn't know where she is. Or *when* it is."

Coral had already become distracted in something else and turned away, humming to herself again.

"She's fine," Sailor growled as she sat up. She pressed a hand to her head. "She just needed to come home."

"Aye," Callum said, "hopefully being home will do her some good. But for now, we have more important things to deal with." He looked up at me, his expression grim.

I nodded. "Something bad is coming this way," I told Mara and Dylan.

"What is it?" Mara asked.

Callum struggled to his feet, groaning as he stood on the wooden leg. "We should get Sailor inside somewhere. Get her some food. Then we can talk."

"I'm fine," Sailor said. She stood as if to prove her point, but she swayed on her feet and stumbled back a step. Dylan started to reach for her, but Callum slipped his hand into Sailor's first.

Dylan's mouth snapped shut and he stepped away, putting distance between himself and the two of them.

"You'll be fine once you sleep and eat," Callum told her gently.

"Fine," Sailor relented, rubbing her forehead with one hand. "I want to go home. To Grandma's."

Dylan and Mara exchanged a look, and I couldn't stop the stab of jealousy that pierced through me. They had spent the last five months together, five months to grow closer while I was thousands of miles away. They had shared experiences and secrets I wasn't a part of. I hated that they could look at each other and convey thoughts without speaking.

But I couldn't think about that now. There wasn't time for jealousy. Domnall would be here soon.

"Let's go to Miss Gale's," I said, turning to lead the way.

Again, I was struck by how empty and silent the streets were as we made our way through Swans Landing. It was the height of summer vacation and the island should have been full of tourists wandering through the shops along Heron Avenue. But most of them were closed, the windows dark and doors boarded up like they were waiting for a hurricane. The whole island had that ghost town feel to it that accompanied a hurricane warning.

"What's going on?" I asked Mara as we led the way toward Miss Gale's house. Dylan and Callum held Sailor between them, helping her walk. Callum's face was twisted into a pained scowl as he walked on his wooden leg, but he didn't complain even once. Coral wandered along at my side, smiling vacantly as she gazed up at the fog over us.

"What do you mean?" Mara asked.

I gestured at the silent landscape around us. Not even seagulls made their usual cries. "Where is everyone?"

Mara shrugged. "The tourists didn't come this year. Without the tourists, the shops didn't reopen for the summer. And without the shops, most people stay at home. It's been like this since you left."

As we turned a corner, we saw that we weren't alone. Kyle McCutcheon and a couple of other guys from school stood on the empty street, bouncing a basketball on the asphalt. They had no net, but they shuffled against each other, trying to block the other's movements.

"Foul," Kyle said, straightening up and tucking the ball under his arm. "You pushed—"

He broke off as he caught sight of us coming down the road toward them. Kyle stared at us, his mouth hanging open. The other two guys—Gabe and Will—turned to see what had Kyle's attention. The three of them looked like gaping fish as they watched us.

"So you're back," Kyle finally said when I was only a few feet from him. He glared at me with dark eyes, a sneer curling the corner of his lips.

"I'm back," I confirmed. Kyle had never been one of my favorite people in Swans Landing. The guy was an idiot and a jackass on top of that. But this wasn't the time for pettiness.

"We came to warn everyone about some people that are coming here," I said. "They want to—"

But Kyle didn't seem interested in hearing my warning. He dribbled the basketball, the thump of the ball against the asphalt echoing loud in the silence around us. "Elizabeth is going to be pissed when she sees you," he snarled. "We all figured we had gotten rid of two of you mutants for good."

Will's gaze fell on Coral and Callum, and he scowled. "Who are they? More freaks?"

Mara gripped my hand tight. "Let's just go."

"Listen to your girl-fish," Kyle said. "I'd hate to beat you like I did your little buddy over there." He nodded toward Dylan, who stood rigid and glaring at Kyle, his face red.

"Come on, Josh," Sailor said. "Let's just go. They deserve whatever Domnall does to them."

Maybe she was right. If Kyle and his friends wanted to be jerks, then maybe I should let them be handed over to Domnall with no warning.

But something wouldn't let me leave without at least trying. I turned back to Kyle and said, "There are people coming who will do everything they have to in order to get what they want. They don't care that you're human, they see it as a weakness. Don't let them near you. Stay in your house. Stay hidden."

Kyle rolled his eyes as he turned away, dribbling the ball again. "I ain't scared of no freaks, Canavan," he told me. "I know how to deal with people like you."

"This isn't a game, Kyle," I said through gritted teeth. "This is serious, and you could seriously be hurt by these people. Or killed. You need to warn as many people as you can."

"Who's ready to play some ball?" Kyle asked the other guys. He hurled the ball at Gabe, hitting him in the stomach. Gabe caught the ball with a grunt and then the three of them launched back into their game.

Frustration welled inside me as I continued past them. I had tried, at least I could say that. I just hoped that the rest of Swans Landing would be a little more open to listening.

* * *

My stomach churned as I led Coral by the hand up the wooden stairs to the bright blue house. Mara walked ahead of us, and Dylan and Callum were last, helping Sailor keep herself steady as she moved up the steps. Neither of them had spoken as we made our way to Miss Gale's house, and they avoided looking at each other.

Mara paused at the door, her hand on the knob.

"How is she?" I asked, keeping my voice low so that Sailor wouldn't overhear.

Mara pressed her lips together, but she shook her head and then opened the door without speaking.

The large combined living room and kitchen was empty when we entered. The lights were off, the house dark. There was no sunlight shining through the skylights overhead. No sounds filled the house. The quiet had settled deep into the cold shadows. It almost felt like no one lived there anymore, like everyone had left.

"Where's Grandma?" Sailor asked, her eyes scanning the room, as if she expected Miss Gale to materialize from the shadows.

"In her room, probably," Dylan said in a solemn tone. He squeezed her hand. "Come on, I'll take you to her."

He glanced quickly at Callum, an obvious sign that he wasn't invited to come along. I looked at Coral, who still held my hand tight and then at Mara. "Maybe I should take Ms. Mooring to see her too," I said. "It might help her remember."

Mara nodded. "I'll wait here with Callum. You go ahead."

Coral followed me quietly as I led her down the hall, following Sailor and Dylan who were just ahead of us. The air in the hall was cold, as if the air conditioner was running needlessly, and I shivered as goosebumps prickled along my arms.

"Miss Gale?" Dylan called, knocking softly on the first door we reached. He turned the knob and the door swung open with only a whispering swish as it brushed across the carpet.

We crowded into the doorway, all four of us looking into the darkened room. A big bed took up most of the space, covered with a thick white comforter.

When my eyes adjusted to the darkness, I could make out the shape under the blanket. My gaze followed the curving slope up to the pillow, to someone who looked too old and too frail to be the woman I had always seen walking around the island. Miss Gale was vivacious and feisty. She always had something to say and wasn't afraid to say it. She served grilled cheese and sweet tea at the food counter in the back of Moody's Variety Store. She lugged home buckets of clams and oysters without asking for help.

But this woman's skin sagged in all the places Miss Gale's never did. Her white hair was strewn loosely across the pillow instead of being bound in its usual braid. The sound of her ragged breathing reached me in the otherwise silent room.

Her eyes were closed and if it wasn't for her breathing, I might think she was already gone.

Sailor stood frozen at my side, her mouth open, but no sound coming out. She stared at her grandmother, unmoving.

But Coral stepped forward, dropping my hand as if she had forgotten I was there.

"Mama?" she asked in a tiny voice.

Miss Gale's eyes opened. Slowly at first, blinking, and then her eyelids snapped open wide as she looked between Coral and Sailor.

"Coral," she croaked. "Sailor. My girls."

Sailor let out a choked sob and then rushed forward, throwing herself onto the bed and wrapping her arms around her grandmother. Coral followed, settling onto the bed on Miss Gale's other side. The three women huddled together, all of them crying.

Dylan and I exchanged a look. This was definitely a woman-only thing. I jerked my chin toward the hall and Dylan nodded. We backed out of the room quietly and I pulled the door closed behind us.

Chapter 4

Mara and Callum sat on stools at the island bar in the middle of Miss Gale's kitchen when Dylan and I found them. I slid into the empty seat next to Mara while Dylan stood on the other side of the island, his arms crossed and his body turned slightly away from Callum.

"Is Sailor well?" Callum asked.

I nodded. "She's with her grandmother. We thought they should be alone right now."

Callum nodded and tapped his fingers on the counter. "It's been a long journey. She should rest." He sounded as tired as he looked. I still felt invigorated by the effects of the song, but I knew that Callum was fighting against the same exhaustion that had overtaken Sailor.

"So what happened?" Mara asked, looking between me and Callum. "You found the finfolk?"

My stomach churned as I thought over the last few months. "We did. Sailor and I made our way to Scotland, to the Orkney Islands. There was a place there called Westray." I met her gaze and smiled. "I took it as a sign, that the island had your name."

She rolled her eyes, but I caught the smile she tried to hide.

Callum and I told them about how we had made our way to Hether Blether and how we were captured by Domnall, the king of the finfolk, and imprisoned for a while. Mara's eyes were locked on me, her expression tense as she listened. Dylan kept his gaze on the floor, but his face was pale as I talked about everything we'd seen and learned and found. The muscles in his jaw twitched when I mentioned how Domnall's men had attacked us before we left.

"So we got away," I finished, letting out a long breath. "We couldn't stay there, not with Domnall intent on coming here. We had to get back to Swans Landing before he did."

"What does he want with us?" Mara asked.

"Domnall wants control," Callum said. "Hether Blether is dying and he thinks that taking control of more finfolk will help. He believes the lost finfolk—your ancestors who came here—broke the protective spell around Hether Blether by leaving. The door to Finfolkaheem closed and our people became susceptible to diseases that had never reached us before."

"Finfolkaheem?" Mara asked.

"The finfolk homeland," I explained. "A city under the ocean."

She ran a hand through her hair, making her curls stick out on one side of your head. "How long do you think we have before they get here?"

Callum shook his head. "Not long. We should prepare your people."

"Prepare them for *what?*" Mara asked. "To fight an invasion of finfolk?"

Callum looked solemnly at her. "Yes, exactly. If you want to keep your island and your life the way it is, you will have to fight for it."

Dylan snorted. "We're not soldiers, we're fisherman. Who do you think is going to fight them?"

"You," Callum told him. "You can use the song's power just like they can."

"But if Domnall already suspects that Sailor and Josh aren't fully finfolk, then maybe he suspects the same thing about the rest of us," Mara said. She looked at Dylan. "How many people here are full finfolk, without *any* human blood?"

Dylan shrugged. "Probably no one. Even those who call themselves fully finfolk have some trace of human blood, several generations back. Most of us are susceptible to the human reaction to the song. Even Lake and Miss Gale. Everyone."

"And the humans wouldn't be able to fight it at all," I added. I slid a salt shaker back and forth across the counter in front of me. It was shaped like a mermaid sitting on a rock, with long blonde hair that fell down her back. Sailor had told me once that her grandmother loved to collect mermaid knickknacks, amused by the way humans depicted us.

"So we're supposed to fight an invasion of fully finfolk people with only humans and mixed breeds," Mara said. She hated the term mixed breeds, so I knew our news had shaken her if she was using it now.

Callum shook his head. "Not all of the people in Hether Blether are fully finfolk."

My head whipped toward him. "What do you mean?"

Callum shrugged. "I told you, the finfolk of Hether Blether used to keep humans on the island. Long ago, before I was born. Most of them were kind of like pets, but others had come willingly and married finfolk. They had children. Some of the finfolk still remaining in Hether Blether today have human blood in them, though they deny it."

Dylan's face was red and his nostrils flared as he looked at Callum. "*Pets?* You kept humans as pets?"

"Not me," Callum corrected him. "It was a long time ago."

Dylan turned his back to Callum, focusing on Mara and me as he leaned over the island, his fists clenched on the countertop. "How do we know we can even trust him? He's one of *them*. For all we know, he got here early so he could tell the others how to find the island."

"Callum has helped us," I answered. Dylan and I had never been very friendly, despite the fact that we both cared about Sailor. The last time I'd seen him before Sailor and I left Swans Landing, he had been furious at Mara and me for sneaking around together behind his back. He liked Mara, and I had known that since her first arrival on the island. It was obvious from the way he looked at her. But I had liked her too, and I didn't want to stay away from her. I couldn't lose her to him.

Dylan curled his lip as he shot a glare at Callum. "These are *his* people coming after us. Let him go out to fight them off."

"Dylan," Mara snapped. "Josh, Sailor, *and* Callum have risked their lives getting back here in time to warn us."

"And doesn't it seem very convenient that they were able to get here before the other finfolk?" Dylan asked, his voice almost a growl. "Maybe he needed to get here first so he could send a signal to the others to let them know exactly where we are. Maybe the plan all along was for him to win our trust and then blindside us later."

Callum stared evenly at Dylan. "I don't know you, and you don't know me. I'm here for Sailor, to protect her."

Dylan's glare darkened at Callum's words.

"This is your home too," Mara told Dylan. "You can fight for it."

Dylan stepped back, his jaw tight. "Whatever. Fight the damned finfolk with your new friend. But don't come to me when he shows who he really is."

"Dylan," Mara started.

But he turned and stormed out of the house, not looking back at us. The door slammed shut behind him, then silence fell over the house again.

Mara sighed. "He's been acting weird the last few months."

I studied her for a moment, then looked down at my hands. "Did anything happen while we were gone?" I held my breath, not wanting to know how she and Dylan had spent the spring and summer, but at the same time, I wanted to hear it from her. If there was anything I should be worried about, I wanted to know now when I could try to distance myself before we fell back into the same spell that had taken over us before.

Mara shook her head. "It's nothing. He's had a rough time with Sailor being gone."

On her other side, Callum traced the line of the tiles on the counter with his thumb.

I cleared my throat. "So we have to figure out a plan."

"What can we do?" Mara asked. "How do we fight them?"

"We'll need more people than just the three of us," Callum said.

I nodded. "We need to gather as many finfolk and humans as we can. We have to let them know about this and get them to work together."

Mara let out a short laugh. "Good luck with that. Things between the humans and finfolk haven't gotten any better. Everyone says this summer is the worst it's ever been. The tourists haven't come. We thought the fishing was picking up in the spring, but then it fell apart again. It's like the fish can't even find their way to the island. Almost like..." Her voice trailed off and she frowned.

"Like what?" I asked.

Worry haunted her eyes. "There have been days when the ferry never comes. It's been happening off and on ever since May. The people on the mainland act like they've never heard of Swans Landing."

"That doesn't make any sense," I said.

"I agree," Mara told me. "Mr. Richter told Dylan the island was being forgotten. Like it was disappearing from the rest of the world."

Over her shoulder, my eyes met Callum's. His mouth was a thin, straight line, his eyes narrowed in thought. Something tickled up my spine. Fear? Foreboding? I wasn't sure.

"That's crazy, right?" Mara asked.

I sucked in a deep breath, then nodded. "Of course. How could a whole island disappear?"

But I already knew how an island could disappear. I had found a disappearing island only three months ago.

But this was Swans Landing, not Hether Blether.

I shook my head. "We can't worry about that right now. We have other things that are more important." I stood and stretched my aching arms. The shark bite had healed and no longer hurt, but my body ached from the weeks of endless swimming. "We need to talk to people soon. Tonight, if we can."

"Maybe we can meet at Moody's," Mara suggested.

I nodded. "That would be great. Do you think you can talk to everyone?"

"Where are you going?" she asked.

I ran a hand over my still damp hair and looked away from her. "I need to go home. To see my mom."

Chapter 5

Mara's footsteps matched mine as we walked down the empty street. I lived only a few blocks over from Miss Gale's house, but then, everything on the island was within walking distance. Mara walked with her hands in the pockets of her sweater, her gaze focused on the ground in front of her feet.

I wanted to hold her hand or kiss her or just touch her. But I kept my arms crossed over my chest to block out the chilly wind. I had thought about the moment I'd see Mara again a hundred times while I was gone. I wanted to tell her I loved her. I knew I did. I had never felt the way I did about her with anyone else. While I was gone, I had worried that maybe it had all been my imagination, just the rush of something new. Maybe Mara had never felt as seriously about me as I did about her. Maybe distance and absence had made me exaggerate the bond between us in my head.

But seeing her again had settled all doubts. The words were there, on the tip of my tongue, but they wouldn't make their way past my lips.

Sailor had said once that Mara and Dylan were probably taking comfort in each other while we were gone. I knew she had said it just to get a reaction from me, but I hated that it still lingered in the back of my mind. Mara and Dylan had acted so strange around each other earlier. They shared looks like they had secrets between them, things they couldn't tell the rest of us. I hated Dylan for getting to have these last five months with Mara while I followed Sailor thousands of miles. It wasn't fair. He was supposed to be the one to go, not me. But when he backed out, I couldn't let Sailor go alone. Finding her mother was supposed to answer questions for both of us.

But had my absence given Dylan the chance to move into my place?

I wished I had the courage to just ask Mara these questions. But I was too much of a coward to know.

"I can come in with you," Mara said when we reached the end of the path to my house. The yard was overgrown with tall weeds that stuck up from the sandy earth. The paint looked as if it had peeled even more since I'd left, and the dark windows stared back at me gloomily.

I shook my head. "That's okay."

"You sure?" Mara asked. She shifted from one foot to the other. The last time Mara and my mom had encountered each other, Mom had thrown a glass at Mara's head.

"It would probably make things worse if you were there," I said.

I knew instantly it had come out the wrong way. Mara's mouth tightened and her forehead creased into a scowl.

"I'm sorry," I said quickly. "I didn't mean—"

"It's fine," Mara said, shaking her head. "You're probably right. I need to go talk to Mr. Moody anyway. I'll see you later."

She waited a moment, but when I didn't move toward her, she turned and walked back down the road, her gaze locked on the ground at her feet. I stood there, watching her leave and wishing I hadn't hesitated. I should have kissed her.

In some ways, I felt years older now than I had before the swim across the ocean. But in this, I felt like a little kid fumbling his way in the dark.

I wanted everything to go back to normal. I wanted the island I had grown up with. I wanted Domnall and his people to disappear. I wanted to be with Mara without worrying about Dylan or people at school or anything else.

I turned toward the house, looking up at the weathered door with the cracked window.

But first, I had to face my mother.

* * *

The keys I had taken with me when I left Swans Landing were long gone, probably still drifting in the boat we'd taken when we left Westray in search of Hether Blether months ago. So I knocked softly on the front door of my own home, unsure whether anyone would even let me in.

After a moment, the door opened and my mom peered out at me. She looked older than she had before. Had those wrinkles around her eyes always been that deep? Did she always have so much gray in her dark hair? Her eyes widened at first when she saw me, but then they narrowed, her lip curling as she looked me up and down.

"I see you didn't die out there after all," she growled.

She stepped back and started to close the door, but I stuck my foot in the way and pushed against it with my hand. "Mom," I said, my voice thick with the sadness inside me. "Can I come in?"

Mom looked at me a moment longer, then turned away and disappeared into the house. She didn't give me an actual invitation, but she left the door open, which was good enough. I stepped into the home I had grown up in, my gaze roaming over the worn, tattered furniture, the dusty shelves and crooked pictures on the walls. A picture of myself as a kid grinned at me. I barely even recognized the person I once was.

I walked slowly toward the kitchen, stepping so softly my feet didn't make any noise on the old floors. Mom stood at the counter, slathering mustard on a piece of bread. She didn't look at me when I entered the room. She moved with short, jerking movements, her shoulders tight.

"We found the finfolk," I said after a long moment of silence.

Mom paused only a fraction of a second before continuing with her sandwich. She replaced the cap on the mustard, tightening it.

"We found Coral Mooring too," I said. "We brought her back home." I knew this news would hurt Mom the most, but she had the right to know that my father's mistress was back.

"You should have stayed there," Mom said as she slapped a piece of bologna onto her bread. "You should have stayed with the rest of your filthy kind."

Her words felt like a slap. I had always known my mom blamed the finfolk for my father's death, just like everyone else on the island did. But she had never referred to me the way she did them. She had made me keep my ability to change a secret from everyone so that they wouldn't know. She had said they would treat me the same way they did the rest of the finfolk. She had said she was protecting me.

But I knew now that she was just hiding her own shame at the fact that she had given birth to a mixed breed.

"Coral might remember what happened the night Dad died," I said. "We had to bring her back home. She's sick—"

"They're *all* sick, Joshua!" Mom whirled around, pointing her butter knife at me, the blade still smeared with yellow mustard. "The whole damned breed is nothing but disgusting, sick fish-people. They're not human. They're an abomination! They shouldn't walk the same earth we do!"

"Mom," I said, holding up my hands to try to calm her. "We're just like you. We can change form, but otherwise we're the same."

I ducked as the knife whirled from her hand, turning end over end until it hit the wall behind me and clattered to the floor. "Get out of my house!" she shrieked.

"This is my home too," I said.

"Not anymore," Mom spat at me, her lip curled in disgust. "I don't want to see you again. You're not my son."

Tears stung my eyes. Her face became a wild blur in my vision. "Fine," I growled, turning away.

I stomped down the hall to my room. I had to get some things before I left. I had played along with Mom's game for years, pretending to be human to make her happy. But that all had ended when I'd left with Sailor. I had made my choice between being finfolk or being human, and Mom wouldn't forgive me for that.

My room looked like someone had torn it apart while I was gone. Clothes were strewn across the floor, spilling out of the dresser drawers. My sheets were torn off the bed and the mattress sat crookedly on the frame. My guitar was smashed, pieces scattered across the floor.

I was familiar with the aftermath of one of Mom's rampages. I had cleaned up enough of them in my lifetime to know what it looked like.

After stuffing some random clothes and toiletries into an old backpack, I changed into jeans and a big black hoodie. It felt good to be in normal clothes again, even if nothing else was normal anymore. I found some old sneakers and shoved my feet inside, not even bothering to lace them.

Mom was sitting at the table, eating her sandwich. She chewed slowly, staring at the wall as if I wasn't there.

I ran a hand over my hair. "I'm going," I said.

Mom kept chewing.

"Mom." I paused, then cleared my throat. "I love you, so I want you to be careful. There is something coming that won't be good for anyone. If you need me, you can find me at Sailor's house or Mara's."

I waited another moment, but she didn't say anything. So I hitched my bag up on my shoulder and walked across the room.

As I reached the doorway, Mom's croaking voice broke the silence.

"You keep playing with that damned fish girl and you'll end up just as dead as your daddy, Joshua."

I stopped, but I didn't look back at her. My nails dug into the strap of my bag.

"I don't know how Dad died," I said, "but I'm going to find out the truth. Even if it takes me years. I'll find out what really happened that night."

Then I left my mom sitting in the kitchen, alone once again.

Chapter 6

Usually only one or two people at a time shopped inside Moody's Variety Store outside of tourist season. Tonight there were more people crowded inside the small shop than I had ever seen at once before. The crowd had gathered at the food counter in the back of the store, where usually Miss Gale could be seen cooking and humming. But the dishes were dusty, and the stove looked as if it hadn't been used in a while.

People sat on every surface available—the barstools, the countertop, an old barrel. The ones who couldn't get a seat stood along the wall or leaned against the display shelves full of duct tape and canned beans and mosquito repellent.

Jim Moody stood behind the counter, his bushy arms crossed over his chest as he studied the crowd in the store. Maybe he was watching to make sure no one stole anything, or maybe he was just uncomfortable being around so many finfolk at once.

It didn't surprise me that most of the crowd in the store was finfolk. Only a few humans were actually friendly to finfolk—Mr. Moody; my guidance counselor from school, Mr. Richter; Mara's friend Claire, who stayed close to Mara's side; Mrs. Kinsey, the local lawyer; and a handful of others. *Not enough.* Not as many as we would need if we hoped to fight back against whatever army Domnall brought with him.

"There are some people missing," Mr. Moody said as he looked over the crowd. "More getting sick, I reckon."

I raised my eyebrows. "Sick?"

His beard twitched as he pressed his lips together. "Strange symptoms, like Gale's. Fatigue, confusion. Humans and finfolk both. Dr. Hanson can't figure it out."

I frowned as this information sank in.

"Go on, boy," Mr. Moody told me, nodding his gray head. "I think that's all that's coming."

I exchanged a glance with Mara, who sat on a barstool next to her dad. Lake's mouth was set in a firm, thin line. I was sure he had already heard some of the details from Mara.

I cleared my throat, trying to get everyone's attention. "Hello," I called out.

But the conversations continued and my voice became lost in the noise.

"If I could have your attention," I said.

When the noise still didn't settle down, Mara shouted, "Shut up and listen!"

All conversation came to an abrupt end and dozens of eyes turned toward me.

I wasn't a public speaker. I had spent my life trying to be as invisible as possible. The urge to burrow into my big hoodie and disappear overwhelmed me, and I had to take a deep breath before going on.

"If you don't know me, I'm Josh Canavan," I said, though the words were unnecessary. Everyone knew everyone else on the island, whether we wanted to or not.

"Oliver's boy," someone said, though I didn't see who.

I nodded. "My dad loved the finfolk. He studied them and tried to learn everything he could about them." I swallowed back the lump in my throat. "Unfortunately, I didn't get the chance to get to know him. But I know if he was still alive, he would have made sure he was here tonight. There is danger coming to the island that will affect all of us, both finfolk and human."

For a second time that day, I told how Sailor and I had found our way to Hether Blether and met the finfolk there. I spoke about the things we had learned from them, the things we had seen with our own eyes and heard them say.

"The king of the finfolk believes that his island is dying out because our ancestors left three hundred years ago," I finished. "He believes that he can save the finfolk race by finding us. By taking over our home and our people, by forcing us to join him. Maybe it's his duty to do what he thinks is best for his people, but it is *our* duty to protect our home from this invasion. We are not all finfolk here. Domnall knows how to use the finfolk songs against humans, even against those of us with a small amount of human blood. He will do whatever he has to in order to get what he wants."

The room fell silent when I stopped speaking. I looked around at the faces that stared back at me, waiting for someone to say something, to have an answer to help us.

Mr. Richter straightened from where he was leaning against the wall. "Why does this Domnall think that coming here will save his people? What exactly is it he wants?"

"He thinks that the mists that protect Hether Blether from the outside world are failing because the song has lost its power," Callum spoke up. He stood, grimacing as he put weight on his wooden leg. We had left Sailor and her mother with Miss Gale, letting them all sleep in Miss Gale's big bed, but Callum had insisted on coming to the meeting. He didn't look as if he had managed to get a nap in the time in between, and dark circles lined his eyes. We were both running on empty.

"Every finfolk carries the power to manipulate things through the song," Callum said. "The song is the melody of the essence inside—the earth, the water, even living creatures.

That explains why humans see things when they hear a finfolk song. It manipulates their minds into creating visions. But the song can also be used to manipulate *places*. The mists that protect Hether Blether were created by the combined song of the finfolk who live there. Whenever they sing, they renew the protective spell. But as the finfolk numbers have diminished on the vanishing isle, the song has lost some of its power. Domnall worries that the island will become visible to human eyes and will be at risk of invasion by them. It's happened before, to an old island where finfolk used to live."

"So he comes here to invade us instead?" Mrs. Kinsey asked.

"How do we fight them?" Mr. Waverly asked. Dylan stood next to his dad, his arms crossed and a deep scowl on his face. I was surprised he had come. He'd stood silently in a corner the whole time, glowering whenever anyone approached him.

Everyone fell silent, waiting for my response. I took a deep breath, knowing that no one would like what I was about to say. "I don't know."

Angry conversations started up again. I held up my hands to try to silence them. "There has to be a way to fight the finfolk, to make them leave Swans Landing," I said. "We just have to figure out what it is."

"Maybe we shouldn't fight them," a man named Piers Rousay said. "Maybe we should let these finfolk have the humans. What have they done for us these last sixteen years anyway?"

Claire's face paled as she stared at the finfolk who agreed with Mr. Rousay. Mara patted Claire's hand reassuringly.

"We're not letting anyone take our home," Lake said, his voice roaring over everyone else's. "This island belongs to both human and finfolk. We'll have to fight together to save it."

"We need more people," I said.

Mr. Moody scratched at his wiry gray beard. "Good luck, son. Many of them ain't likely to take orders from no finfolk."

"What about from you?" I asked.

Mr. Moody shrugged. "Can't make no promises. Some of them are stubborn. Harry Connors, in particular."

Mara's gaze shot across the room, locking on Dylan's, who stared back at her. Something in my gut twisted as unspoken words passed between them.

"We have to try," I said, pushing away thoughts of whatever was going on between Mara and Dylan. It wasn't the biggest thing to worry about right now.

"Do you have any idea when these finfolk will be coming?" Mr. Richter asked.

Callum shook his head. "We swam as fast as we could to try to get ahead. We don't know how far behind us they are."

Lake stood, pushing his long hair out of his eyes. "Then we have to be prepared, for whenever they show up."

"I'll talk to as many people as I can," Mr. Richter said. "I'll try to get them to listen."

"The rest of us should do what we can to fight, whether or not we have help," Lake said.

Everyone stood and began breaking off into groups or leaving. It seemed that the meeting was over, though I didn't know what we had really accomplished. We still had no idea how to fight Domnall.

"How did things go?" Mara asked, reaching across the counter to touch my hand. "With your mom?"

We hadn't had a chance to talk again before the meeting, so I hadn't been able to tell her anything.

"Not as well as I'd hoped," I said. "But pretty much what I expected. She kicked me out."

Mara's eyebrows shot up. "*What?*"

"I guess I'm homeless now." The words didn't bother me as much as I expected them to. I had known how mom would react back when I decided to leave. I had been homeless for the last five months.

"You can stay at my house," Mara said.

I looked across the room to where Lake stood talking with Mr. Richter. Mara's dad and I had never really talked. Before anyone knew the truth about me, I had spent my life avoiding crossing paths with other finfolk as much as possible, as if maybe they could figure out the truth about me if they got too close. I had no idea what he thought of me, or of the fact that I was involved with his daughter.

"You sure that's a good idea?" I asked.

Mara nodded. "It'll be fine."

Chapter 7

"Absolutely not."

Mara glared at her father, crossing her arms. "Why not?"

Lake shot her a look like she had gone insane. "Because you're seventeen and you are not moving your boyfriend into my house."

I shifted from one foot the other, staring at the toes of my dirty sneakers. It was pretty clear how Mara's dad felt about me now.

"Where is he supposed to go?" Mara asked. "His mom threw him out."

"I'm very sorry about that, Josh," Lake said. "But I have to be Mara's dad here, and I'm not comfortable with the two of you living under the same roof. I know what it's like to be a teenager."

"We are capable of restraining ourselves without tearing each other's clothes off every second," Mara snapped.

Lake's neck reddened and his nostrils flared.

"What if I promise to keep at least three feet between us at all times?" I asked, cracking a grin to try to lighten the tension in the air. It didn't work, judging from the way Lake's eyes flashed.

Mara let out an annoyed huff. "*Now* you want to be my dad. Just in time to piss me off."

Lake scowled. "Watch your language. It's my final decision. He'll have to stay somewhere else."

Mara opened her mouth to say something, but I reached out and grabbed her hand. "It's fine," I said. Mara and Lake had a rocky relationship, and I didn't want to be the cause of any new problems between them. There was no reason to make him more upset than he already was. I nodded to Lake. "I understand. I'll find some place else to go."

Mara shot her dad one last glare before she followed me out the door. We sat down on the top step, our sides pressed close together. Mara leaned her head on my shoulder. Twilight had fallen and the half moon hung in the sky behind the thick clouds. The island was quiet and still. In the peacefulness around us, it was hard to imagine that something bad was coming.

"Sorry about Lake," Mara told me.

"It's okay," I assured her. "Maybe I can stay with Sailor. Callum and I can snuggle together on the couch."

Mara's mouth curled into a slight smile. "So about Callum," she said. "What's the deal with him?"

"What do you mean?" I asked.

She lifted her head, her eyebrows raised. "What's going on between him and Sailor?"

I shrugged. "They became close. That's all I really know."

"Are they dating?"

"Yes, they went out to the movies last week," I said dryly.

Mara punched my arm. "You know what I mean."

"Does it matter?" I asked, kicking at a loose rock on the step near my foot.

"Not to me," Mara said. "But I think it matters to Dylan."

My forehead creased into a deep scowl. "And whatever concerns Dylan concerns you?" I snapped.

Mara pulled away slightly. I felt her gaze on me, but I didn't turn to look at her.

"Dylan is my friend," she said.

I let out a bitter laugh. "Is that all he is?"

"Are you accusing me of something?"

"You two have had five months alone together," I said. I didn't want to fight with Mara, but I couldn't hold the words back. Everything that had happened that day had settled heavy on my shoulders and I was suffocating under the pressure. My nerves were too frayed and on edge. I needed a release, to vent something before I exploded.

"I saw the way you two looked at each other," I went on. "Why don't you tell me what happened while I was gone?"

"What about what you've been doing?" Mara asked. "How do I know you didn't find your own Scottish finfolk like Sailor did?"

She scowled at me with those golden brown eyes I had thought about for months. I wanted to take back everything. I was tired and had missed her too much.

"I'm sorry," I said softly. "I didn't mean that. I'm just tired."

We sat there silent for a long time, before Mara leaned her head against my shoulder again.

"Dylan is my friend," she said. "*Just* my friend. I've waited five months for you to come back to me." She sighed. "But I thought it would be different when you did. I didn't think that we'd be waiting for an invasion of finfolk."

I slipped my arm around her back and pulled her close to me, kissing the top of her head. The wind lifted strands of her hair, brushing them against my face.

"I'll do everything to protect you," I told her.

Mara turned her head toward me, smiling up at me. "And what about you? Don't you need protecting?"

I laughed. "Are you volunteering?"

"I'm not a damsel in distress, you know," Mara said. "If some finfolk king thinks he's coming here to take over just because he wants to, he hasn't met me yet. I'm the girl who punched Elizabeth Connors in the face, remember?"

"I don't think I'll ever forget that. You were kind of scary. And awesome. But mostly scary."

Mara punched my leg gently. "That's right. So just wait until these finfolk get here. I'll make them wish they'd never left Hether Blether."

I leaned down to kiss her, enjoying the feel of her warm lips against mine and hoping that she was right.

* * *

My neck felt like I'd slept while contorted into a pretzel. I stared up at a gray sky visible through the skylight high overhead. Crystal prisms hung from fishing line under the skylights, but there wasn't enough sunlight for them to reflect it anywhere.

I groaned as I stretched, my feet hitting the end of the couch and my arms hitting the other end. My head was turned at a painful angle and I had to slowly ease myself around into a sitting position. I rubbed at my neck, trying to work out the kinks.

Voices behind me caught my attention and I turned, blinking as I peered toward the kitchen area. Two figures sat at the island bar, their backs to me and their heads bent together, one red and one brown.

I padded over to the kitchen, rolling my head around to stretch out my neck. "Morning," I groaned.

Sailor and Callum pulled away from each other slightly as I joined them. They had empty cereal bowls in front of them and a box of Corn Flakes on the counter next to a half-empty gallon of milk. Miss Gale was known across the island for her home cooking, so the fact that she wasn't in here making one of her famous breakfasts spoke volumes about her condition.

"How are you?" I asked, studying Sailor. She looked better than she had in a long time. Some color had returned to her cheeks and her eyes didn't show as much exhaustion as they had the day before.

"I'm good," Sailor told me. "Hungry though." She reached for the Corn Flakes and poured herself another bowl.

"That's her third bowl," Callum told me with a smile. "I like a lass with a good appetite."

I found a bowl and a spoon and joined them for breakfast. "I hope you slept better than I did," I said.

Callum had insisted on taking the love seat and letting me have the longer couch, claiming that he didn't need as much room as I did. I doubted that was true, since we were about the same height and build, except for the fact that Callum had one less limb than I did.

"Probably not," he said. "But I was too tired to care much."

My stomach growled as I chewed my first spoonful of cereal. I hadn't thought about how hungry I was until then. I had been too busy to eat after we'd arrived in Swans Landing, and then once I made it back to Sailor's house, I was so exhausted I wanted to sleep for days. I felt like I could eat a few bowls of cereal myself.

"So Callum told me how the meeting went," Sailor said through a mouthful of cereal. "Do you think anyone will be able to convince the rest of the humans to help us?"

I shrugged. "I don't know. If they're all like my mom, probably not. But I don't see what other option we have. We need as many people fighting back against Domnall as we can get."

"I don't know how much help the humans will be," Callum said, shaking his head. "They'll be easily susceptible to the song's effects, and Domnall knows that. He will use it against them."

"Is there anything else the song can do?" I asked. "Is there a way we can use it to protect them? To manipulate their reaction to the song with a different one?"

"Not that I've ever heard," Callum said. "The song was only meant to help finfolk. We've never really been interested

43

in trying to protect humans, so we wouldn't have tried to develop songs for them."

I hated that the stories about finfolk were true. I had read all the books and websites about finfolk that I could find, and they all said the same thing: Finfolk were cruel creatures and they used their powers to trick humans into following them to their deaths, or else kidnapped them to keep as pets. I had never wanted to believe it. The finfolk in Swans Landing seemed like ordinary people.

But if these stories were true, if finfolk could be that cruel, was there something inside me that could be just as bad as them? Did that kind of cruelty live in the blood within me that gave me the ability to change?

I gulped down the last of the cereal and drained the milk from the bowl. I wiped my mouth and then stood, looking Callum up and down. He still wore the tattered, dirty robe he'd been given back in Hether Blether.

"I think I have some clothes that might fit you," I said. "Look in my bag. There should be some jeans and T-shirts. Sorry I don't have extra shoes."

Callum inclined his head once. "That is fine. Thank you."

"Where are you going?" Sailor asked as she watched me deposit my bowl in the sink.

I ran a hand over my hair. "I'm going to talk to some old friends," I said. "See if I can convince them to join us."

Sailor raised her eyebrows. "Humans?" she asked.

I nodded. "I have to let them know what's coming and try to make them see that joining together is the only option we have."

Chapter 8

I shoved my hands deep into the pocket of my hoodie as I stood on the Moorings' front porch and looked at the ominous fog that hung low in the sky. It was way too cold for August. Things just weren't right here on the island, something other than the threat that lurked out in the ocean. The island reminded me of Hether Blether, and that thought chilled me all the way to the bone.

As I walked down the stairs, a movement out of the corner of my eye made me stop in my tracks. I peered into the shadows underneath the house. Like most other houses in Swans Landing, it was raised off the ground by wooden pilings, to protect it from flooding during hurricanes or other rough storms. Most people used the area under their homes as storage for things like lawnmowers and yard tools. Miss Gale kept her belongings a little more neatly organized than most people did, but there was still a lot under there and a lot of places that someone could hide.

A chill prickled the back of my neck. I felt unseen eyes watching me. I moved down the steps and then walked slowly toward the area under the house, my eyes scanning every inch.

Was Domnall here already? Had he arrived while we were sleeping and now either he or one of his people waited under the house for us?

I reached the first wooden piling, where a shovel leaned against an old cabinet. I reached for the shovel, my eyes never leaving the space under the house.

"I know you're here," I called out, trying not to sound as nervous as I felt. "Come out now."

There was movement to my right as a large shape rose from behind another cabinet. Brandishing my weapon, I took off after the figure, leaping over a push lawnmower.

The person's feet got tangled up in some old fishing baskets, and the figure sprawled across the sand, sliding to a stop just a few feet from me. I raced over there, pointing the shovel at the figure's back as I kicked him over to get a look at his face.

Harry Connors stared up at me, his face red around his bushy beard.

"What the hell are you doing here?" I asked.

Mr. Connors's gaze flicked to the shovel still pointed at him and then back at me. He pushed the shovel out of his face as he sat up. "What're you planning to do with that, boy? Dig my grave?"

"A grave is too good for you. You deserve to be tossed out in the ocean for the fish." Mr. Connors had always been the loudest voice speaking out against the finfolk. He never missed a chance to remind me that they had killed my father.

But I lowered my weapon as he stood.

"I'd heard you were back in town." Mr. Connors looked me over, crossing his thick arms over his chest. "You don't look better for all of the trouble you've caused. You should be ashamed, leaving your mama alone like that while you chased after those abominations."

My lip curled. "I'm only going to ask you this one more time. What are you doing here, sneaking around Miss Gale's house?"

Mr. Connors's face turned a deep crimson, but he glared back at me. "I came to see for myself that the rumors were true. That you and your bastard sister were back, and you brought her whore mama with you."

I raised the shovel again, pointing the tip at Mr. Connors's throat. "You might want to think carefully about what you say next."

Mr. Connors wrinkled his nose and pushed the shovel away again. "You ain't a killer, boy. You were raised to be one of us. You *could* be one of us again. We'd overlook your little problem in the water. We'd do it for your mama's sake. All you have to do is stop running around with these freaks and come back to us."

A way out. A way to pretend at being human again, like I had done all my life.

A half-life, Mara had called it. A life that ignored the part of my father living inside me.

"No, thanks," I said.

"They'll kill you, just like they did your daddy."

I gripped the handle of the shovel so tight I felt splinters digging into my palms. "Do you even realize what's going on here? People are coming to take our home. They'll use whatever power they have to get you out of their way. You're *nothing* to them, unless you work with us to fight them."

Mr. Connors stepped back, putting distance between us. "I ain't joining your kind, boy. Out here, we have our own way of dealing with problems." His hand moved to the holster at his hip, resting on the grip of a silver handgun.

I sighed. I knew Mr. Connors was a lost cause. He hated the finfolk too much to listen to reason.

"Where's Elizabeth?" I asked him.

Mr. Connors's eyes flashed and he pointed a thick finger at me. "You stay away from Lizzie."

"I need to talk to her."

"You need to keep the hell away from my daughter!" Mr. Connors roared, spittle flying out of his mouth. "I won't have you contaminating her mind with your singing. If I find you near her, I will take care of you myself, boy."

With that, he turned and stomped across the yard, kicking up sand as he walked.

* * *

There were only so many places a person could hide in an island as small as Swans Landing. I knew Elizabeth didn't like to spend a lot of time at home, especially during the summer. Even though it didn't really feel like summer that day, I decided to start my search at the beach.

I spotted two figures under the remains of the broken pier. A hurricane had destroyed half of the pier a decade ago, but it had never been rebuilt. What remained was technically off limits, but that never stopped anyone from going out on the pier when they wanted.

Jackie and Elizabeth were sitting on a big beach towel under the broken structure, far enough away from the water that it didn't reach them whenever the waves rolled in.

I approached them from behind.

"You've been acting so weird lately," Jackie complained. "What's going on with you?"

"Nothing," Elizabeth snapped, crossing her arms over her chest. "Nothing's going on."

"Well, you've certainly been in perpetual bad mood," Jackie muttered.

They were so absorbed in their own conversation, they didn't know I was there until I spoke.

"Hey."

Their heads whipped around, craning to look up at me. Elizabeth's eyes widened for a moment, her mouth falling open slightly. Jackie just sneered.

"Look what the tide brought in," Jackie said, nudging Elizabeth's arm with her elbow.

Elizabeth looked at me for a long time without speaking, then she said, "So you didn't get eaten by a shark after all."

I cringed, remembering the feel of the shark's teeth ripping into my arm. "Not quite," I said. I crouched down next to them. "Look, I need to talk to you about something very important."

Jackie snorted and pulled her knees up to her chest. "We don't talk to people like you."

I kept my gaze locked on Elizabeth's green eyes. We had been sort of friends once, as much as anyone could call someone like Elizabeth Connors their friend. I knew she had liked me for a long time, though I had never felt the same way. And she was probably mad at me for choosing Mara and turning my back on a human life. But I hoped that maybe, somewhere inside, she still thought of me as the same guy she had always known.

But Elizabeth's expression hardened, her forehead scrunching into deep lines. "Jackie's right. We don't talk to your kind."

She turned her face away from me, looking out at the crashing waves.

"Elizabeth," I said in a stern voice, "you have to listen. This affects you too. There are people coming here who will hurt you—"

"Are you deaf or just stupid?" Jackie snapped. "We're not talking to you."

I resisted the urge to grab them both and shake them as hard as I could. "I'm trying to help you!" I shouted.

Elizabeth sneered at me. "We don't need help from mutant freaks. You made your choice. You're not one of us."

"It's time to get over the stupid feud on this island," I said. "This place belongs to all of us, and we need to work together. These people who are coming don't care that you hate us. They'll take control of your mind and do what they want with you."

"Do you hear an annoying buzzing sound?" Jackie asked Elizabeth. She shot me a deep glare. "It's giving me a headache."

Elizabeth scrambled to her feet, brushing sand off her legs. "Come on, Jackie. Let's get out of here. The stench is too rotten today."

I gritted my teeth together as they made their way down the beach, leaving me crouched on the sand under the pier. I hoped that maybe Mr. Richter or someone else had had better luck than I was having.

Chapter 9

Someone stood at the bottom of the stairs to the Mooring house when I returned after my failed attempt at speaking to Elizabeth. It was too tall and thin to be Mr. Connors, and as I got closer I recognized the long dark hair.

"Mr. Westray?" I asked.

Lake jumped, his hand clutching the golden locket he wore around his neck as he turned to look at me. "Oh, Josh," he said, sounding a little breathless. "I didn't see you there. Hi."

"Hi," I said, nodding to him.

Lake didn't make any movement to go up the steps, or get out of the way so that I could pass, so I stood there, facing him. His response to Mara asking if I could stay with them flashed through my memory. I probably wasn't at the top of his list of favorite people right now. I shifted from one foot the other, trying to think of something to say.

"Um," I said at last. "So did you want to come in?" I gestured toward the house at the top of the stairs.

"Oh." Lake blinked up at the house, as if trying to figure out what he was doing there. He coughed and pushed his hair out of his eyes. "I don't know if I should. Maybe I should go home. I have things to do."

But still, he didn't move from where he stood, one hand on the wooden railing.

"Come inside," I urged him. He let me pass to go up the steps ahead of him. When I was halfway up, I heard his steps following me.

Sailor had given me a spare key before I'd left, so I let myself in. The house was quiet and dark. I left the front door open for Lake to follow as I walked farther inside the house.

"Sailor?" I called. "You home?"

There was no answer, but I found a note on the counter in Sailor's handwriting. *Gone to find Callum something for his leg. Back soon.*

A footstep behind me let me know that Lake had come in. I turned to him, waving the note. "Looks like Sailor isn't here," I said. "Miss Gale is probably asleep."

Lake ran a hand through his hair. His gaze was locked on the edge of the counter, as if it was the most fascinating thing he had seen all day. "What about…Coral? Is she here?"

I raised my eyebrows. "She might be. I can check."

"I don't want to bother her," Lake said quickly. "I mean, if she's asleep, let her sleep. I just…wanted to see her."

He looked like a lost kid, like he was unsure where he was and was ready to take off at any moment.

"I'll go check," I told him.

Coral sat in the little room at the end of the hall that must have been hers once, before she left Swans Landing. The walls were painted a soft yellow and had old posters of actors and musicians that were now considered ancient covering them. She was at her desk in front of the window, just like she usually was whenever Sailor and I would go to see her in Hether Blether. Her head was bent over a paper and her hand moved quickly, sketching in lines and shadows.

"Ms. Mooring?" I asked gently, hoping I wouldn't startle her.

Coral looked up at me and blinked a few times. Her face showed no recognition. It was just blank. She didn't even seem to think I was my father today.

When she didn't answer me, I said, "There's someone here to see you."

She didn't respond, so I backed down the hall to where Lake waited in the kitchen. He tapped his fingers on the edge of the counter, sighing a little as he waited.

"You can go in," I told him. "But she's kind of…She doesn't always remember people. And she doesn't know what year it is, I don't think."

His expression became even more fearful at my words. I motioned for him to follow me and we walked softly down the hall.

"Ms. Mooring?" I asked, tapping lightly on the door. She still sat at the desk, but she stared out the window in front of her, her hands paused over the drawing on the desk. "Lake Westray is here to see you."

Lake stepped into the room, his eyes darting around nervously, as if something might jump out at him at any moment. He ran a hand through his hair, pushing it back from his eyes.

Coral looked over her shoulder at him, her expression blank. Finally, she smiled a little.

"I thought you were too busy with your new girlfriend to come see an old friend," Coral said.

Lake glanced at me and I shrugged. As I had warned him, Coral didn't seem to know what year it was. Ever since we'd found her in Hether Blether, her mind had jumped from one point in the past to another, with moments of clarity very few and far in between. She seemed to be stuck mostly in the time frame right before she left Swans Landing.

Right before my father died.

I wanted to ask her about that night, to see if she could tell me anything. I didn't want to confuse or upset her even more than she already was, but Coral Mooring might be the only person who could tell me about my dad's last moments since my mom refused to talk about him. I had decided to wait until she had a day of more clarity, when she didn't seem so confused or lost in time. That day hadn't yet arrived.

"Coral," Lake said as he perched himself on the corner of her bed closest to the desk. "How are you feeling?"

Coral looked him up and down, a smirk etched across her face. "You're going to marry her, aren't you?"

Lake blinked a few times before he said, "Do you mean—"

"Don't deny it," Coral snapped. "I see it in your face. You've spent the whole summer with her. No time for your old friend. You'll leave me just like *he* did. He's having a baby, did you know that? All that talk about loving me and wanting to spend his life with me." She laughed bitterly. "It was a lie. It's always a lie."

I stepped back into the hall, wanting to disappear. She must have been talking about my dad. They fell in love when my mom was pregnant with me.

I tried to understand what would make my father have an affair. What would make him turn his back on his pregnant wife? How could he have been so in love with my mom one day, enough to start a family with her, and then decide he loved someone else months later?

I wanted to believe he was a good man. I had to believe that he was, or else I had to face the fact that the blood that flowed in him was the same blood that flowed in me.

I didn't want to be someone that could cause so much pain to the people I cared about.

I left Lake and Coral sitting there while I walked back down the hall. I stopped to check in on Miss Gale, who was asleep, her soft snores drifting toward me. My footsteps made no noise on the soft carpet as I approached the bed.

Miss Gale's eyes were closed tight. Her skin was still too white, her cheeks sagging on her bones.

"Miss Gale?" I whispered.

There was no response from the bed. I stood there for a moment, thinking that I should probably go and let her sleep. But I wanted some company, even if the other person didn't know I was there.

I sat down in the chair by the bed. At first, I kept my hands in my lap, but then I reached forward and slipped my hand into Miss Gale's small one. She seemed so much tinier than she always had before. She wasn't a very big woman, but she had a huge personality that made up for it.

I could tell how much Sailor loved Miss Gale whenever she talked about her, even when her grandmother frustrated her. I imagined what it would be like to have someone like Miss Gale looking after me as I grew up, how different it would have been from the childhood I knew, taking care of my mom during her episodes that made her violent or confused.

Miss Gale wasn't my grandmother, but maybe, just for this moment, I could pretend she was.

She stirred and I started to pull my hand away, but her grip tightened around my fingers. Her eyes fluttered open and she blinked a few times.

"Josh?" she croaked.

My cheeks burned. "I'm sorry, I didn't mean to wake you."

Miss Gale shook her head a little. "You didn't." She didn't comment on my hand in hers, but she continued to hold on, rubbing her thumb over my fingers. "What's been happening while I've been asleep?"

How much had Sailor told her grandmother? Did Miss Gale know about Domnall? I thought about telling her everything, how Sailor had brought Callum back from Scotland, how we were waiting for an invasion that we didn't even know how to prepare for.

But already, her eyelids were drooping closed again and she sighed heavily.

I rubbed a hand over her head, smoothing back her soft white hair. "Go back to sleep," I said gently. "Everything's fine."

I left her in the dark room and went back to the kitchen.

I had just finished a peanut butter sandwich when Lake came into the room. His hair looked like even more of a tangled mess than usual and his eyes were bloodshot. I didn't want to think about whether he'd been crying. It was too weird.

Lake cleared his throat. "Let me know if Coral needs anything," he said, avoiding my gaze. "Or any of you. I'll do what I can to help."

I nodded. "I will."

He picked at the edge of the counter with his thumbnail. "I'm really sorry for not letting you stay with Mara and me. But I'm a dad, and one day, when you become one, you'll understand my position."

I nodded. "It's no problem. I get it."

He looked like he wanted to say more, but then he let out a deep breath and nodded. "Okay. I'll see you later then."

He started toward the door, but then I said, "I love her, you know."

My neck burned when Lake looked back at me. I dropped my gaze to the crumbs of my sandwich on the plate in front of me. "I wouldn't do anything to hurt her or anything she didn't want to do."

Lake was silent for a moment, then he said, "I know you wouldn't, Josh. But what scares me is how much she would *want* to do with you. I see the way she looks at you and the way you look at her. I know how that feels. And sometimes, when you're that much in love, you don't think about the consequences before you act. You don't think about how hard it might be later."

Sadness washed over his face and I wondered if he was really talking about Mara and me, or if he was remembering how he felt with Mara's mom.

"I know with the way things are right now and with everything the two of you have gone through, it's tempting to jump into things because you think there might not be a tomorrow." Lake sighed. "I just want you to really know what you're getting into before you act."

With that he walked out the door, leaving me picking at the crumbs on my plate.

Chapter 10

I broke the surface, shaking salt water from my eyes. I looked back to the shore, where a blonde figure still stood.

"See anything?" I called.

It was probably useless to shout. The wind whipped hard over the ocean and Dylan didn't seem as if he could hear my question.

It would be easier if he would just get into the water. But he refused, despite the fact that Lake had assigned us to swim the area around Pirate's Cove as part of our watch. It had been suggested that the finfolk could already be here, waiting underwater for the perfect moment to come ashore, whenever that might be. So we were divided into pairs and given areas around the island to search, both ocean and sound sides. None of us thought it was likely that the finfolk would come from the sound, but we wanted to cover all bases just in case.

Not that we could actually see anything. It was dark and murky in the water. If the finfolk were under there somewhere, they could easily hide.

A large swell washed over me, submerging me for a moment before I rose above the surface again. The water was too rough. I could barely keep myself from being carried back to shore.

I had hoped to swim with Mara, since we hadn't had a chance to swim together in the two days that I'd been back. But Lake had paired me with Dylan instead. Was he intentionally keeping Mara and me from spending too much time alone, or did he just like to torment his daughter's boyfriend?

The current tossed me toward shore again before I was able to fight against it and stay near the place where I had surfaced.

"This is pointless," I growled as I fought against the crashing waves. We couldn't keep searching every inch of the ocean. I hadn't even been out there long and I was already exhausted.

I sighed as I scanned over the water again. Still nothing. I might as well join Dylan back on the sand.

Not too far out from the shore, the current became strange. Water pushed at me from all sides, all directions. If I let myself go, I started to turn in a dizzying pattern. I panted as I struggled to get out of the swirling water.

"Dylan!" I called out. I didn't know if he could hear me, but I didn't have time to wait for a rescue that might not come.

I arced down into the water. The current was even stronger below and even more confusing as it pushed first one way and then another. I let myself drift with the water instead of fighting it, surrendering to the violent current.

When the current pushed me to the left, I waited as long as I dared and then torpedoed out of the stream, flicking my tail fin hard and pumping my arms. I swam as far and as hard as I could, until finally my fingers brushed sand.

I panted as I grabbed the beach towel I had left on shore and began drying myself in the cold wind. "Thanks for the help," I muttered.

Dylan rolled his eyes. "You won't drown," he reminded me. "So you weren't in that much trouble."

"What was that anyway?" I asked.

"It looked like a whirlpool."

"You ever seen one this close to the island?"

"No," Dylan said, frowning as he looked back at the water.

"We should tell the others," I said. "So they'll know to stay away from it."

"Maybe if we're lucky these finfolk will be caught up in it," Dylan said.

I shook water out of my ears. "Maybe. We don't have any other options right now."

Dylan's expression hardened. "If these people are as dangerous as you say they are, then we maybe we should take more extreme measures."

I raised my eyebrows. "Like what?"

"We have one of them here already," Dylan said, his eyes narrowed. "Why don't we find ways to make him talk? Tell us what he knows?"

"Callum?" I shook my head. "I told you, Callum isn't helping Domnall. He's on our side. He doesn't know any more than we do."

Dylan laughed, a short harsh sound. "That's what you think right now. But how well do you really know this guy? He willingly took you and Sailor straight into danger. If he knew how bad these finfolk were, why did he even take you to them? He risked your lives, and you're lucky you got out."

"He took us there because we asked him to," I said. "Callum has helped us the whole time. He warned us not to let them know we were part human. He warned us not to trust them. He's on our side."

"No one is ever on the side you think they are," Dylan said. He glared at me, then turned toward the trees.

I got dressed and then followed him down the narrow path through the trees, back to civilization. We walked in silence for a while, both of us keeping our distance from each other.

"So what's your real problem with Callum?" I asked finally.

Dylan's head whipped toward me, his light blue eyes narrowed. "What's that supposed to mean?"

"Do you distrust Callum because he's from Hether Blether, or because Sailor likes him?"

Dylan's jaw clenched, but he didn't say anything.

"Sailor has been in love with you for years," I said. "It's funny that now that she's found someone else, you get all jealous."

Dylan stopped, whirling around to face me. "I am not jealous of that creep. Sailor is my friend. I still feel the same way about her that I always have. But I don't like *him*. I don't see any reason I should believe he's not just like the rest of his people."

"What is it then?" I asked. "You're acting like you want to beat the hell out of him."

"I'd like to beat the hell out of someone around here all right, and not just Callum." Dylan sneered at me before turning and walking down the road.

I laughed. "Me? Go ahead then. You've waited this long to do it, get it out. I'm sorry if you think I stole Mara from you, but as far as I know, she's free to like anyone she wants. It just didn't turn out to be you."

Dylan kicked at a crushed can on the street. "Yeah, too bad she has terrible taste in guys."

We didn't talk for a few minutes. I walked a few steps behind him and he never looked back.

"So what happened while I was gone?" I asked finally. "Did you make a move on Mara and she shot you down? Is that why you're so pissed off these days?"

Dylan's eyes flashed as he glanced over his shoulder at me. "You'd love to hear that, wouldn't you? What if I said I made a move and she *didn't* turn me down?"

My fists curled tight at my sides. He was trying to make me mad, I knew. Mara had already said nothing had happened and I trusted her.

"What if she ended up in my bed again, only this time, she didn't run away?" Dylan said with a sneer. "Maybe I gave her what you couldn't."

I clenched my teeth, ignoring his words. "We could be friends, you know," I said. "I have no issue with you. We're both finfolk and we're in this together. We should team up."

"Get lost," Dylan said.

"You just hate to lose, don't you? You lost Mara and now you're losing Sailor to Callum. Sorry the whole world doesn't revolve around you, Waverly. It's called free will. People can do what they want."

Now Dylan stopped and faced me, his neck reddening and his fists clenched at his sides. "You know what my problem with you is, Canavan? You make everyone lie to me. Mara sneaked around with you, even after spending the night in my bed. She went right back to you and never said a word to me, letting me think that maybe what had happened between us meant something. And you made Sailor lie to me for years. She knew exactly what you were and who you were, and she never said a thing to me about it." He glared at me. "I don't know what it is about you, but you cause trouble just by being around. I can't trust anyone because of you."

I stepped toward him, but Dylan backed away. "Don't," he said, holding up his hands. "We did our job, now I'm done with you."

He left me standing there, watching as he disappeared down the sidewalk. We were on the edge of the town, near the shops that had never reopened for summer due to the lack of tourists. The darkened windows looked out at me, like ghosts watching my movements.

A step behind me caught my attention and I spun around, my fists clenched and body rigid.

"Oh," I said, trying to push the tension out of my body. "You."

Elizabeth Connors stood nearby, her arms crossed and her eyebrows raised. "Don't sound so excited."

"What are you doing here?" I asked.

Elizabeth shrugged. "Free country. I can go where I want." Her gaze drifted over my shoulder. "What were you and Dylan arguing about?"

"Nothing that concerns you," I snapped.

Something passed across Elizabeth's face. Disappointment or regret, something that made her mouth turn down quickly before it was replaced by her usual sneer.

"I thought you weren't talking to me," I said.

Elizabeth tossed her hair over her shoulder. "I'm sure he's thrilled you're back. Dylan probably hoped you'd disappear in the Bermuda Triangle, so he could have Mara all to himself. Don't you think they were pretty cozy here, all alone without you and your little sister to keep them company? To keep watch over them?" She smiled wickedly. "What kind of trouble do you think Dylan might have gotten himself into during his summer vacation if you had never come back?"

I wouldn't let Elizabeth see what effect her words had on me. I knew her game. I had seen her play it too many times.

"Why aren't you calling him Fish Boy?" I asked.

Elizabeth blinked quickly, her sneer wiped away. "What?"

"I've never heard you call Dylan by his name," I said, narrowing my eyes at her. "You never call any of the finfolk by their names."

Elizabeth glared at me, her hair whipping around her head in the breeze. Fallen leaves and bits of trash tumbled down the street around her as she glared at me.

"You should have stayed gone," she spat at me before turning and marching away.

* * *

Since I was already out in town, I walked farther north along Heron Avenue to the squat blue building that served as the Sand Dollar Restaurant and Inn.

The sign was turned to the OPEN side, so I pushed on the glass paneled door and stepped inside the dimly lit room. Large windows lined the walls, but the sky outside was so gray and cloudy that there wasn't much sunlight filtering into the dining room. There were no customers at the tables, so the bell on the door jingled in the silent room as I entered.

The swinging door to the kitchen opened and my former boss, Mr. Jasper, strode into the room. He was a older man, with thick gray hair and deep lines in his face. Those lines deepened as he spotted me, his mouth turned into a frown.

"What're you doing here?" he growled, his dark eyes looking me up and down.

"I came back yesterday," I said.

"So I heard." Mr. Jasper crossed his arms. "We're not hiring, so don't think you can get your job back."

I didn't expect to. I had left without notice, and I had figured that bridge was long burned.

"I didn't come for my job," I said. "I came to talk to you."

Mr. Jasper turned toward the kitchen. "I have nothing to say to you," he growled as he disappeared through the door. It swung back and forth a few times, making a soft swishing sound in the silence.

I couldn't say I was surprised at this reaction. Mr. Jasper was never a very warm person, and I knew that he didn't like finfolk very much. Now that he knew what I was, he would never welcome me with open arms.

The kitchen was cold and quiet when I stepped through the door. My sneakers squeaked on the tiled floor. Usually, the kitchen at the Sand Dollar was full of activity, pots and pans cooking on stoves and chefs dashing back and forth. But today, it was still. The only person in the room was Luis, the head chef who usually worked alone only during the off-season. For the summer, there should have been at least four cooks with him, helping to manage the rush of tourists.

Luis lifted his head from a magazine spread open on the counter in front of him. He studied me, but didn't speak.

"Hi," I said at last. "Bet you didn't expect to see me again."

Luis shrugged. "I figured you'd come back eventually. Mr. Jasper hoped otherwise, I think."

I glanced at the door in the corner that led to the offices, where Mr. Jasper had probably escaped to avoid me. "I see he hasn't changed much since I've been gone," I said.

"What did you expect?" Luis asked. "You disappeared without notice. You not only left your mother, but you left your job. And then Mr. Jasper heard what people were saying about you, about what you really are. You lied to him, for a long time. He had *respected* you, Josh. You were a hard worker, a good young man. Now he doesn't know who you are."

"I'm still the same person I've always been," I said. "Finfolk or human, I'm still me."

Luis looked at me for a moment. Then he pressed his lips together in a straight line and shook his head. "I don't know if that's true."

I sighed. I didn't come here to argue with anyone or defend what I'd done five months ago. There were more important things to worry about.

"Have you heard what's going on?" I asked. "What's coming?"

"Those creatures that people say are coming?" He nodded curtly and snapped his magazine shut. "I've heard."

Luis wasn't a native Swanser. He had grown up in Texas and had only moved to Swans Landing about three years ago. Until now, I wasn't even sure that he knew about finfolk. It wasn't something that people talked often about with outsiders. Even though he'd been here for a while now, Luis would always be a Woodser, an outsider, in most people's eyes.

"You need to listen to it and take it seriously," I told him. "These people aren't going to care who they have to hurt to get what they want. They're dangerous and they know how to do things that you can't fight against."

Luis narrowed his eyes. "If these people are finfolk, like you, then why are you warning me about them? Shouldn't you stick with your own kind?"

My lip curled in disgust. "They are not my kind. These people are completely different from the finfolk here in Swans Landing. I'm not like them."

Luis stood, his eyebrows raised. "You lie, you hurt people. Seems that you're not that much different."

I opened my mouth, but I couldn't deny what Luis had said. I had lied, to a lot of people. And I had hurt more people than I'd ever wanted to.

But I was not like Domnall. I knew that deep in my gut. I would never be like him. I would never hurt people the way he did to get what I wanted.

"I should go," I said.

Luis nodded. "You probably should."

At the door, I paused, my hand on the painted wood. I looked back at Luis, who was now polishing utensils by the stove.

"Please just be careful," I said. "And keep an eye on Mr. Jasper."

Then I pushed the door open and left the kitchen, walking across the silent dining room to the front door of the Sand Dollar. I had done what I could to help the humans of Swans Landing, but I hoped it would be enough.

Chapter 11

Sailor inspected a jar of pickles and then tossed it into the basket she had set on the floor by her feet. "Do you like olives?" she asked me.

"Not really." I leaned against the shelf of ketchup and other condiments and sighed. "Sailor, are you even listening to me?"

"No," she said, sticking her tongue out at me. She nudged the basket with her foot, moving it down the aisle to the display of rice and pasta. The basket was already nearly overflowing and it didn't look like she was done shopping yet. The cabinets at Miss Gale's house were looking pretty empty, most likely due to the fact that Miss Gale hadn't left her house in months.

"You need to talk to Dylan," I told her again. "He's upset about you bringing Callum back with you. I think you should go talk to him about it."

Sailor shrugged. "It's not my problem if he's jealous now. He didn't care to take notice of me all these years. I moved on and found someone else. If he doesn't like it, whatever. I don't care." But the edge to her voice told me she did care, even as she scowled at a bag of white rice before tossing it into the basket too.

"Look," I said, "it's not my business who you want to be with. If it's Dylan or Callum, that's up to you. I'm not getting into the middle of your relationships. But there's something bigger at stake here, and we all need to work together if we want to survive. So you need to talk to Dylan and get him to trust that Callum is on our side. I'm afraid of what might happen if we start fighting with each other."

Sailor sighed. "I'll try to talk to him. But I can't make any promises that he'll listen. Dylan can be stubborn sometimes, when he wants to be."

"Tell me about it," I muttered. "You're not the one who had to go out on watch with him this morning. I'm glad Lake agreed to let me go alone next time."

"When are you on duty again?" Sailor asked.

I looked up at the dusty old clock hanging over the door of Moody's Variety Store. "Half an hour," I said. "I'll be there until tonight. So you don't have to worry about me for dinner."

Sailor frowned. "I'm not worried about feeding you. You're welcome to what we have. Jim told me to take what we need."

"It's all right," I said. "I'm used to not eating much. I can survive on peanut butter sandwiches, remember?"

Sailor made a face and I laughed. She had probably had enough peanut butter sandwiches while we were in Scotland to last her the next year.

The bell over the door jingled and we both turned to see who had come in. Mr. Connors stood in the doorway, his dark eyes locked on us.

"Tell me Elizabeth's not with him," Sailor muttered, turning back toward the shelf in front of her.

"I don't think so," I said. "But he's bad enough by himself."

I hoped Mr. Connors would go on about his business, but his heavy footsteps on the wooden floor sounded as if they were coming straight for us. He stopped only a few steps away and I felt his eyes scanning the two of us.

"Shopping?" Mr. Connors said. "I thought your kind liked to just steal the catches right out of my crab pots. Easy dinner for you, right?"

Ignore him, I thought, trying to send a silent message to Sailor. She seemed to be unusually interested in a jar of spaghetti sauce.

"I got a visitor this morning," Mr. Connors said. "That fool guidance counselor from your school. Seems you all brain-washed him into believing your stories about *bad finfolk* coming to take over. He tried to tell me not to go out on my boat anymore. Like I have a choice. I don't fish, my family ain't got no food. Not that it matters, with your kind stealing my catches anyway."

"You should listen to Mr. Richter," I said. "These finfolk could come at any time. You don't want to be out there, facing them alone."

Mr. Connors sneered at me. "I ain't scared of nobody, boy, least of all freaks like you. I've dealt with the trash of your kind long enough to know that the only good finfolk is a dead one. Like your daddy."

I clenched my teeth, but I forced myself not to slam my fist into his jaw.

His gaze flicked toward Sailor and he looked her up and down, his lip curling. "Too bad you found your mama still alive, girl. Just when we thought we'd rid this island of one piece of trash, you had to go and bring her back."

I reached out to grab Sailor and hold her back before she could lunge at Mr. Connors, but another figure stepped between us. Jim Moody stared at Mr. Connors, an ancient double barrel shotgun clutched in his hands.

"Harry," Mr. Moody said, his eyes never leaving the other man's face. "I'll have to ask you leave my store. I ain't tolerating harassment of my customers."

Mr. Connors's face twisted into a snarl. "Ain't I your customer, Jim? Or you gone soft over these freaks too?"

The shotgun rose steadily as Mr. Moody aimed it at Mr. Connors's chest. "I'll ask one more time, Harry. Leave, or you'll never make it out of here in one piece."

"Don't tell me you've grown a conscience now," Mr. Connors snarled. "She may be your granddaughter, but she's just as much an abomination as the rest of them. You made a mistake long ago with her grandma. We can all understand that, the way they use their songs to manipulate and control us. But if you don't watch yourself, Jim, the rest of us might not be so understanding anymore."

Mr. Moody raised the shotgun until the barrel was pointed at Mr. Connors's head. "I'll give you three seconds to get the hell out of my store."

Mr. Connors opened his mouth, then snapped it shut. He shot us all one last glare before he stomped out of the store.

Mr. Moody lowered his gun, his shoulders sagging. Then he turned and looked at Sailor.

"If he bothers you again, let me know," Mr. Moody said. He nodded once to me, then started back down the aisle, swinging the gun at his side.

"Thanks," Sailor said. She didn't look at him, but stared at the jar of spaghetti sauce she rolled back and forth between her hands.

Mr. Moody paused and glanced at her, then at the floor. "How is Gale? And…your mama?"

Sailor set the jar back on the shelf and then bent to pick up her shopping basket. "You should come see for yourself," she said. She hitched the basket onto her arm and then disappeared out the door, the bell jingling behind her.

* * *

"It's freezing out here," Mara said as she sat down on the edge of my beach towel. She offered me a thermos. "I brought you some soup."

The plastic bottle felt good on my cold fingers and I cupped my hands around it as I smiled gratefully at her. "Thanks," I said.

Mara leaned close to me, slipping her arm through my elbow. "No problem. It sucks you got one of the late shifts."

There were three of us at different points along the ocean side of the island, working in eight hour shifts. I had volunteered to take an overnight shift, but Lake insisted that the adults would do that. I had bitten my tongue to keep from pointing out that my eighteenth birthday had already passed and therefore, I was technically an adult.

"When do you think they'll come?" Mara asked. The last bits of sunlight were fading behind the foggy clouds and we couldn't see very far into the water. But I peered into the distance as hard as I could, my eyes watching for any shape that seemed out of the ordinary.

"I don't know," I answered. "I don't think it will be much longer. Even without them knowing the exact way, they couldn't have gotten too far behind."

Mara's grip on my arm tightened. "I keep hoping they won't come. Maybe they'll get lost."

"Or eaten by sharks?" I asked, with a smirk.

Mara laughed. "We can only hope."

I shared the hot soup with her, though I noticed she didn't drink much. Mara had had an early day shift at Pirate's Cove. I figured Lake had arranged that to put her at the least likely place for the finfolk to appear. My shift was near the lighthouse, where we all expected the finfolk to come. The light would guide them directly to our shores, but there was no way we could turn it off without risking other boats and ships running aground.

When Mr. Richter arrived to take over the watch for me, Mara and I walked back toward her house. The streets were still quiet and empty. It felt like mid-winter, not late summer.

"Why is it so cold and cloudy?" I asked. I slipped my arm around Mara's shoulders and pulled her closer to me for warmth.

"It's been this way since winter," Mara said. "It's like it never really went away."

I looked up at the mist swirling in the sky over our heads. "It reminds me of Hether Blether," I said. Something tickled in the back of my mind as I spoke this thought. Like I was missing something I had overlooked. But no matter how hard I searched my thoughts, I couldn't figure out what it was.

"What do you think these finfolk will do when they get here?" Mara asked. "Will they make us all go back to Hether Blether with them? Will they move here?"

I shook my head. "I'm not sure exactly what Domnall wants to do. He says he wants to save the finfolk from dying out, but if he just wants more people in Hether Blether, then we could give directions to anyone who wants to get there. His coming here is not a good sign. He has no sympathy for humans."

We reached Mara's door and paused on the steps, facing each other. I leaned my forehead against hers, closing my eyes and enjoying the warmth of her body.

"I wish everything could stay like this," she said. "Just you and me."

I kissed her, wrapping my arms tight around her waist and pressing her into me. I had wanted this, all those months I was gone. I wanted her, all of her.

But then I thought of my dad and I pulled away.

"What's wrong?" Mara asked.

"Nothing," I said. I couldn't meet her eyes and when I tried to kiss her again, she moved out of the way.

"Don't tell me nothing," Mara said. "I'm the queen of 'nothing.' Something's wrong. I can see it on your face."

72

I traced a crack in the wooden railing next to me with my thumb. "Do you ever wonder what makes people attracted to each other?"

"You mean besides the prospect of sex?" Mara grinned.

My cheeks burned hot, but I went on.

"I mean, it all seems so fickle, doesn't it? How can you be in love one day and want nothing to do with each other the next?"

Mara's eyes narrowed as she studied me. "What is this about, Josh?" Her voice held a worried tone.

"My parents," I said, and Mara's expression relaxed a bit.

"What about them?" she asked.

I ran a hand over my hair. "I have to believe that at some point, my parents were in love. They got married, they made me. There must have been some kind of attraction there. So if that was true, why did my dad fall in love with someone else so easily?"

"Your dad made a conscious choice. He knew what he was doing and he could have chosen not to act on it."

"What made him decide to throw away his marriage for another woman? Was it the human part of him, or was it the finfolk trapped inside?" The questions haunted me every second.

"It's not a human or a finfolk thing, it's a personal decision. He could have kept his distance from Sailor's mom, or he could have divorced your mom first."

"It just seems like it's too easy to hurt someone you think you love," I said.

"What's really wrong with you?" Mara asked. "There's more you're not telling me."

I closed my eyes, letting out a long breath. "What if I'm like him? I don't want to hurt you, but what if I can't stop myself from doing it one day?"

Mara gripped my chin, turning my face toward her so I could look into her eyes. "Josh, you are not your dad.

Whatever he did, it was his choice. It doesn't mean you'll do the same things he did."

I knew she was right. The words sounded so reasonable. But I couldn't chase away the feeling inside me, like there was something waiting to fall apart because I'd make the wrong choice.

"I just wish I could have known what he was thinking," I whispered.

Mara leaned forward, pressing her lips to mine. I let myself give in to her kiss, pushing away thoughts of my parents and everyone else. I wanted this moment, this time we had to ourselves.

She reached behind her and unlocked the door to her house. It was dark. Her dad was probably already out at his station at the beach for the night watch. We stumbled through the doorway, our lips never breaking the hungry kiss.

I pushed her against the wall, one hand slipping under her shirt to touch the soft skin of her stomach. She sighed softly and pressed against the back of my head, pulling me into her like she couldn't get close enough to me.

"What do you see when you hear the song?" Mara asked, her lips close to my ear. She hummed a few notes of the water song, causing gold bursts to erupt along the edges of my vision.

"You," I told her. "Always you."

But when I glanced to the side, where the gold bursts were strongest, the hazy form I saw there wasn't Mara, but a face I had only seen in photographs.

My father.

I stepped back, wrenching my hands from Mara's body. My pulse throbbed throughout my body. I felt the absence of her as if part of myself had been torn away.

Mara blinked at me, her lips swollen and her eyes shining in the dim room. "What is it?" she asked, panting a little.

I scrubbed at my eyes, trying to chase away the remains of the song's effects. "I should go," I said.

Mara looked at the door, then at the darkened room behind us. "You don't have to. Lake won't be back until morning."

Her tone held the promise of something I had only imagined happening. I couldn't deny that I wanted nothing more than to stay with her all night. My entire body ached with the need to stay.

But Lake's words echoed in my head. *Sometimes you don't think about the consequences before you act. You don't think about how hard it might be later.*

It was already hard enough right now. I didn't want to mess things up. I didn't want to repeat mistakes my dad had made by jumping into things without thinking.

I kissed her softly, then pulled away. "No," I said. "I should go."

She leaned against the door as I descended the stairs. I paused and sucked in a deep breath of cool air, then let it out slowly, watching as my breath mixed into the mists in the air. I must have been insane or stupid. Possibly both. My body screamed at me to go back to her, even as my head told me that I had the same blood as my father and would make the same mistakes he did.

Don't walk away from this chance, Canavan, a voice in my head said. When would Mara and I have a night alone like this again? If I walked away now, I knew I would regret it tomorrow. If Mara ran to Dylan because I blew her off at a moment like this, I wouldn't even blame her.

But I couldn't hook up with Mara now, when my mind was too preoccupied. I wanted to be sure, I wanted to know that it was right. I didn't want it to be something we did just because we were afraid we wouldn't have the chance again, or because I was trying to prove something to myself.

I didn't want it to be hard later. When it happened, I wanted no consequences, no regrets for both of us.

Mara still stood in the doorway at the top of the steps. I gave her one last wave, then I forced myself to walk away.

Chapter 12

The house was quiet when I walked in, which wasn't unusual. I was getting used to the quiet around the Mooring house.

I peeked into the hall and saw the doors of the three bedrooms were all shut. There was light coming from the crack under Sailor's door and I could hear her muffled voice drift toward me, followed by Callum's. I could only imagine what they might be doing in there, locked away with no supervision.

In the living room, I flopped down onto the couch and sighed. How was it fair that Sailor could move her boyfriend into her house while Mara and I had to keep our distance? I wondered what Miss Gale would think about Callum staying there if she were well enough to notice. Maybe I should tell her what was going on.

No, I wouldn't do that. It was Sailor's business, and if she wanted her boyfriend or whatever Callum was to her in her room, then why should I care? She always did what she wanted anyway.

I bit my lip, feeling guilty about that thought. Sailor was still my half-sister. She had always been the one person who was there for me, who accepted me as I really was.

A sound at the front door startled me. I waited, straining my ears to listen. There it was again. A footstep, just outside the front door.

The hairs on the back of my neck prickled. I didn't know if it was Domnall and the finfolk or else Mr. Connors sneaking around the house again, but neither was a good option.

I tiptoed across the room, slipping up to the wall next to the door. I peeked out the window at the front of the house, but I didn't see anyone. My body was rigid, my legs tensed to spring at the first sign of trouble. I needed a weapon. A bat or something. An umbrella stand sat in the corner behind the door and I carefully eased a green umbrella from the group, wielding it over my head like a club.

Taking a deep breath, I grabbed the knob and snatched the door open, letting out a choking growl when I saw a figure standing on the front stoop.

"It's me, boy!" a voice growled from behind the raised hands.

I lowered my umbrella, blinking as my gaze took in Mr. Moody huddled away from me.

"What are you doing here?" I asked. I tossed the umbrella aside, feeling silly for carrying it.

Mr. Moody scratched at his chin. "I came to see Gale. Like Sailor told me I should."

"It's kind of late," I pointed out.

Mr. Moody looked up at the night sky, like he had just noticed the darkness around him. "Oh. Right. I can come back tomorrow."

"No, it's okay." I stepped back to let him in. "Miss Gale is in bed, but you can go see her. She's always in bed these days."

Mr. Moody stood just inside the door, looking around the house like he was far outside of his comfort zone. His eyes took in the crystals hanging from the skylights over us and then the blue walls. He dug his hands deep into his pockets.

A step in the hallway caught my attention and I turned to see Sailor, with Callum right behind her. Sailor's mouth fell open when she spotted Mr. Moody.

"What are you doing here?" she asked.

Mr. Moody cleared his throat. "I, uh, I came to see your grandma."

Sailor scowled. "Why?"

Mr. Moody scratched his chin. "I thought I'd take your advice."

Sailor stepped forward, but kept the island counter between herself and her grandfather. "No, I mean, why *now?* All these years and you've never come. Now she's sick and suddenly you want to be here?"

Callum put a hand on Sailor's shoulder, but she didn't acknowledge him.

Mr. Moody's beard twitched as he swallowed. "I've always wanted to be here, Sailor."

Her eyes turned glassy as she looked at him. "Then why weren't you?"

"Sailor," Callum said soothingly as he rubbed his hands over her arms. "You should lie down for a while. You're tired and you could use a good rest."

Sailor glared across the room at her grandfather, who rubbed at his chin, his gaze on the floor. Finally he lifted his eyes to her and said, "I'm only human, Sailor. I make mistakes. But I'm not the only one."

Callum whispered in Sailor's ear and she let him pull her away from the counter. They disappeared back down the hall and then a moment later, I heard the click of her bedroom door closing again.

I shoved my hands deep into the pocket of my hoodie. Mr. Moody exhaled a long, ragged breath. He didn't speak and the silence grew thicker as minutes passed.

Finally, I dared to speak. "Do you want me to see if Miss Gale is awake?" I asked.

Mr. Moody nodded. "That would be good, son. Thank you."

He followed me as I walked down the hall to Miss Gale's room. There was no light coming from under Sailor's door. Maybe Callum had convinced her to lie down. She was on edge a lot lately. I didn't know if it was just the lingering exhaustion from our long swim or the stress of waiting for something to happen. Or maybe it was the situation she had gotten herself into with Callum and Dylan.

I tapped softly on Miss Gale's door as I opened it. The room was dark and still. I could make out the shape of Miss Gale on the bed, but she didn't respond when I called her name.

"I think she's asleep," I told Mr. Moody. I motioned for him to come in. "But she probably wouldn't mind if you woke her."

Mr. Moody walked across the room slowly, as if it was hard to get one foot in front of the other. His back was stooped more than usual and he reached out a trembling hand toward Miss Gale when he reached the bed. He looked at her for a moment, his beard twitching as he pressed his lips together.

I started to back out of the room, but he said, "You don't have to go, boy. I wouldn't mind the company."

Mr. Moody sat down in the chair next to the bed, which Sailor or Coral usually occupied. I wasn't sure what to do with myself, so I stood near the door, my hands in the pockets of my hoodie.

Mr. Moody didn't speak for a long time. He just sat there, looking at Miss Gale as she slept. Her soft breathing was the only sound in the darkened room.

"If she were awake," Mr. Moody said at last, "she'd tell me I was an old fool." He laughed a little. "Just like she always does."

I smiled. I knew Miss Gale enough to know that she always said what was on her mind, no matter what it was. She'd tell you honestly how she felt about you.

"Maybe I am an old fool," he continued. "Maybe that's why I've never stopped loving her, even when she told me I shouldn't." He stroked her long white hair, a small smile on his face. "Did you know, boy, that I asked her to marry me?"

"No," I said softly. "I didn't know that."

"I've asked her that question probably a hundred times over the last forty years."

Ouch. Poor guy. "She always says no?" I asked.

Mr. Moody shook his head. "She's never said yes or no. She just always tells me that she can't let me tie myself to her with the life she lives. She doesn't want me to watch her going into a world I can't follow." He leaned forward, lowering his voice. "But I'm still here, Gale, and I'm still waiting for an answer."

If this were a movie, one of those cheesy happily ever after things, Miss Gale would have woken up right then and told Mr. Moody that she would marry him.

But it wasn't a movie, and Miss Gale's eyes stayed closed, her breathing even and soft.

"I am an old fool," Mr. Moody said. "For her. Always for her."

I swallowed as I watched him gaze at her. His eyes had this look like he had never seen anyone else as beautiful as her. Even after forty years of pushing him away, his love had never faded.

It gave me hope to know that sometimes even our own actions couldn't destroy a love like that.

Chapter 13

"Callum Murchadh?" the nurse called, butchering the pronunciation of his last name. She looked up from the file folder, raising her eyebrows at the three of us.

Sailor and I helped Callum to his feet and across the waiting room toward the door into the exam area. Other people slumped in the chairs around the waiting room, their gazes following as we moved. An old man coughed, wheezing loudly in the otherwise silent room. A little girl lay across three seats, her face pale and her breathing heavy.

Callum eased himself onto the examination table, his wooden leg tapping against the metal as he moved.

"Doctor Hansen will be with you soon," the nurse told us as she backed out of the door, as if she couldn't move fast enough.

Sailor sat down in the only available chair, while I leaned against the wall, my arms crossed.

"I'll be glad to get rid of this bloody thing," Callum said, glaring down at his wooden leg. "Hopefully this doctor of yours can give me a real prosthetic."

"Doctor Hansen is the best doctor on the island," I told him.

"The *only* doctor on the island," Sailor said with a smirk.

I nodded. "That too."

"Is she…" Callum frowned, his forehead creasing. "How does she feel about finfolk?"

Sailor and I exchanged a glance. Honestly, I didn't know. I had always been to her pretending to be human. I had no experience with Dr. Hansen's opinions on finfolk.

"I guess we'll see," I said as the door opened.

Dr. Hansen was in her mid-forties, with sandy blonde hair pulled back into a ponytail. She smiled awkwardly at us as she closed the door behind her.

"Hello," she said, extending a hand toward Callum. "I'm Dr. Hansen."

Her smile was strained, her expression tight. It was easy to see that she wasn't entirely comfortable around us.

"Hello," Callum said with a nod. "Thank you for seeing me, even though I don't have medical insurance."

Dr. Hansen opened the file folder and scanned the page. "Everyone has the right to medical care in my office."

"Even finfolk?" Sailor asked.

Dr. Hansen fumbled and a paper fell from her hand, fluttering to the floor. She bent to scoop it up, avoiding our gazes. "Yes, well, you're human enough in anatomy, aren't you? I don't proclaim to be an expert in finfolk, but I'll do what I can." She cleared her throat and then turned to Callum. "Now, let's look at that leg."

Dr. Hansen examined Callum's leg. She removed the crudely made prosthetic and then studied the scarred skin where his leg had been cut off by Domnall four years ago.

"What happened here?" Dr. Hansen asked in a soft tone. Her fingers poked timidly at the stump of Callum's leg, as if she were afraid of hurting him now.

"I was punished," Callum said. "For doing something that resulted in the death of my sister."

Dr. Hansen's eyes snapped up to meet his gaze. "Cutting off your leg is a proper punishment among your people?"

"Not commonly, but the person who did it felt that it was justified."

Dr. Hansen pressed her lips together as she examined Callum's leg again. "The person who did this," she began, "is he the one people say is coming here?"

"Yes," I said. "His name is Domnall, and he's the king of the finfolk on an island called Hether Blether. He is leading some of his people here. And he will not let anyone stand in his way. *Everyone* here is in danger. Look at what he did to Callum. Don't think that he won't do the same to you."

Dr. Hansen's hands trembled and she pulled away from Callum. She turned back to the file folder on the table, scribbling down some notes. "I can get you a real prosthetic," she said, her voice cracking a little as she spoke. "You really need a custom made one for the best fit, but this one will do for now, until you can get to the mainland one day to a specialist."

"Thank you," Callum said.

Dr. Hansen rubbed her forehead, letting out a long breath. "Just doing my job." She looked tired and I thought of the people in the waiting room.

"Have you been really busy lately?" I asked.

"More so than usual," Dr. Hansen said. "Especially considering there are no tourists on the island right now. I don't usually see this much business from the locals during the summer, when everyone is supposed to be busy working."

"What's wrong with them?" Sailor asked.

Dr. Hansen shook her head. "I wish I knew. It's not a virus. Not an infection of any kind. I can find no logical cause for this illness. At first, it was only the older people falling ill, but recently, I've seen young children come in with the same symptoms. Coughing, wheezing, confusion, exhaustion. I can't explain it."

Sailor and I exchanged a look. Symptoms just like Miss Gale's.

"Is this affecting both humans and finfolk?" I asked.

"From what I can tell, it is," Dr. Hansen said. "Although most finfolk aren't coming in for treatment. They're a bit more stubborn than the humans sometimes." She cracked a half-smile. "No offense intended."

I returned her smile. "None taken."

Dr. Hansen called for the nurse and instructed her to get a prosthetic from the supply closet. The nurse returned with the metal leg, casting anxious glances at the three of us as she backed out of the room again.

Once Callum was fitted with the new prosthetic and had taken a few test steps around the room, he thanked Dr. Hansen. Dr. Hansen led us back to the front, to the checkout desk.

"Let me know if you have any problems or discomfort," Dr. Hansen told Callum.

Callum nodded. "Aye, thank you again."

Dr. Hansen smiled and nodded good-bye before turning to head back to the door marked OFFICE.

"Dr. Hansen," I called. She stopped and looked back at me. I felt the eyes of everyone in the waiting room on me, as well as the eyes of the receptionist behind the desk.

"Please think about what we told you," I said, loud enough for everyone to hear. "These people that are coming are very dangerous. We all need to work together in order to stop them."

Dr. Hansen glanced at the patients seated around the room, then her eyes met mine again. She nodded. "I will, Josh. Thank you for talking to me."

I only hoped that she, along with everyone else watching us, would take the warnings seriously.

* * *

I dug into my bag and pulled out the finfolk key that we had taken from Hether Blether. It didn't even look like a key

84

at all. It was just a piece of twisted iron. But it had come from Finfolkaheem, the ancient finfolk city under the sea. It was the key that had let us find Hether Blether months ago. It was the one thing Coral had insisted on getting before we left the island. The thing we had risked our lives for.

And for what exactly? Coral said my dad had told her it was important, but I couldn't figure out why. We were far away from Hether Blether now, and I had no intention of ever going back. In this part of the world, the key was probably nothing more than a piece of metal.

"If you have any secrets that can help us," I said to the metal in my hand, "now is the time to reveal them."

"Oliver."

I jumped, nearly dropping the key in my lap. A face peeked around the corner from the hall, wide green eyes blinking at me.

"Ms. Mooring?" I asked. "I thought you were asleep."

"I kept them for you, Oliver," Coral said. She glanced around the room and then tiptoed toward me, her skin ghostly white in the glow of the single lamp that lit the room. "I kept them safe, just like you told me."

I pinched the bridge of my nose. "I'm sorry, Ms. Mooring, but you have me confused with someone else. I'm not Oliver. I'm Josh, his son."

She reached for my hand, tugging my arm. "I'll show you where I hid them."

She was surprisingly strong for a woman who was still so thin. I dropped the key back into my bag and stood, letting her pull me down the hall. We passed the closed doors of Sailor's room and Miss Gale's, and then headed into Coral's darkened room at the end.

"Over here," she whispered, hurrying toward the corner behind her bed. She knelt on the floor, pulling at the carpet.

I knelt next to her and helped her pull the carpet away from the tacks that held it in place. Coral dug her fingers into the edge of the floor, just under the little gap where it met the wall.

A square chunk of the floor came up easily and she tossed it aside. A dark hole gaped up at us from the corner of her floor. I looked at Coral and she smiled wide at me, nodding.

"I kept them for you," she said again. "Just like you told me to."

I hesitated, wondering what exactly it was she had kept hidden like this. Then I leaned forward and reached into the hole. I tried not to think about spiders or snakes or other things that liked to bite that may be hidden inside. My fingers found a cold metal box, and I pulled it out, sitting it in my lap.

The box was old and dirty, the edges starting to rust, but the latch clicked open when I pressed it. I opened the lid and reached to turn on the lamp on Coral's nightstand.

Yellowed paper and worn notebooks filled the inside of the box. I took the paper off the top of the stack and unfolded it carefully, staring down at the writing. It wasn't the words on the page that made a chill creep down my spine. I couldn't even focus enough to read anything the paper said.

But the handwriting—I knew the handwriting. I had seen it once before, in a notebook my mom had caught me reading when I was thirteen. I had found it in an old box at our house, tucked away in the back of a closet. The handwriting of a ghost that had haunted my life, the last remnants of a man I'd never known.

My mom had burned the notebook after she caught me reading it. She had burned everything in the box, and I thought anything that was left of my father aside from a couple of photographs had disappeared in that blaze.

My eyes met Coral's and she nodded, her smile stretching from one ear to the other. "Just like you told me, Oliver," she said. "I hid them. I kept them safe."

Tears stung my eyes and she became blurry in my vision. I reached over and squeezed her hand. "Thank you, Coral," I said. "You did great."

My heart drummed against my ribs as I looked down at my dad's writing once again.

Chapter 14

"You sure you want me to read these?" Mara flipped through a notebook and gave me a hesitant look.

We sat on the torn couch at her house, about three hours before I was supposed to start my shift on beach watch. The box of papers and notebooks sat between us.

"There's a lot to read and not much time to read it," I said. "My dad must have known something about what was going on around here. He visited the Orkney Islands himself at one point, and I believe he was searching for Hether Blether. I thought that he wanted to go there just because of his obsession with finfolk, but maybe it was more than that. He told Coral that she needed to find the key. We have it, now we just need to know why it was important."

I yawned and rubbed at one eye. I had stayed up half the night, reading the papers. My dad's handwriting wasn't easy to read. He scrawled a lot, as though he couldn't write fast enough to get his thoughts out. In some places, it had taken me long minutes of staring to figure out a word.

I opened a notebook to where I had left off the night before. It was written only a few months before I was born.

April 9 - The fishing season has come back, but as noted last year, there is a distinct decline in the population. The fishermen I've traveled with noted lower catches of sea mullets and red drum. No bluefish have appeared at all so far this season.

It is still early, but if my previous observations hold true, the population will not increase as expected the further we head into the season. My temperature readings on the water in various locations today were as follows:

Lighthouse: 48° F

Pirate's Cove: 49°F

Water temperatures are remaining below expected average.

Most of the entries in the notebook were like this. Notes on weather, the water temperatures, and fish populations.

"My dad noticed that the fish populations were decreasing eighteen years ago," I commented. "But no one else seems to have really taken it seriously except in the last few years."

Mara shrugged. "Maybe everyone thought it was just a temporary thing. Like, a few bad years, followed by good years. Isn't that how it usually works?"

If it was, it didn't seem that it worked that way anymore. Not in Swans Landing, anyway. We'd had eighteen straight years of declining fish populations and lower water temperatures. It had caused people to leave the island in search of better jobs and for tourists to stop coming. But what exactly was causing it?

I flipped through the notebook, my eyes scanning over the words until one caught my eye: Coral.

July 13 - Coral Mooring has become somewhat of an assistant to me in my studies. She is helpful to have around, since she can swim farther and deeper than I can. She gives me first hand reports on the topography of the ocean floor around the island and the numbers of schools she sees down there. The reports are not any better than what I've been able to observe on my own.

I read back over the short entry, trying to pick up any hidden thoughts my dad didn't write down. But it seemed so innocent, a partnership in studying the water around the island. My dad had been a marine biologist, so he spent his life studying the ocean. I hadn't read anything so far that would tell me why he fell in love with someone else. Because they spent so much time together? Was that all it took to forget your vow to someone else?

I looked up and studied Mara's profile as she read over the papers in her hand, her forehead scrunched in concentration. Maybe I should have asked Sailor to read these with me. It was her father too. But a part of me wanted to keep this part of our dad to myself for now, at least until I had some answers I could give her.

"He mentioned you here," Mara said quietly, casting a quick glance at me.

I sat up, my body tense. "He did?"

Mara cleared her throat and read from the page. "August second. I'm a father. Silvia delivered our son, Joshua Oliver Canavan, at three twenty-one this morning. He is the most perfect thing I have ever seen. I left Silvia and Joshua at the hospital on the mainland and came back to the island once I saw that they were settled in comfortably and healthy.

"Why am I back here, sitting on this boat alone when I should be with my wife and son? Joshua's birth made me even more determined to find out what is causing the decline of our island. There is something at work here that none of us can explain and I fear for the future. For my son's future. I have to find a way to fix this, for him."

I gritted my teeth together so hard that my jaw ached. My eyes burned with hot tears that wouldn't fall.

"Josh?" Mara asked, reaching out to touch my knee.

"It's funny, isn't it?" I asked, my gaze locked on the notebook in my lap. "He wanted to make things better for me, but he didn't spend what little time he had left with me. I was only a few hours old and already he was back out there on the water. And all of it was for what? Just so he could end up getting himself killed over a woman he could never really be with? Over people that he would never be a part of despite the blood that ran in his veins?"

We fell silent for a moment. The house creaked and popped as it settled around us.

"Maybe he couldn't help feeling the way he did," Mara spoke up. "Maybe he tried to fight it, but it was instinct."

I blinked quickly, but my vision became blurred through the tears. "He had more finfolk blood in him than I did, but he couldn't change, no matter how much time he spent in the ocean. And the one thing that killed him is the one thing that I can't do. I can't drown, *ever*. That's the only thing my dad ever gave me, besides these notebooks that aren't telling me a damn thing I need to know!" I flung the notebook across the room. It hit the wall and then fell to the floor, the pages fanned out and the cover bent.

Mara moved across the couch, wrapping her arms around me. I bit my lip until I tasted blood and buried my nose in her neck. She smelled so good and the feel of her body next to mine made me buzz with energy from head to toe.

I pulled back, my lips finding hers. I didn't want to think about my dad or the finfolk or anything else right then. I wanted this, I wanted her. Always. I wanted to be as close as possible to her, closer than I'd ever been to anyone. I wanted her to make me forget.

My hands moved under her shirt, my fingers tracing the lines of her ribs.

Mara pulled back, breaking the kiss. "Not like this," she said.

I blinked, my mind clouded with hunger for her. "What?"

She pushed herself away from me, shaking her head. "Not like this. We're not having sex just because you're upset and don't want to think about your dad." She crossed her arms as she looked at me, her eyes wide. "I want to, I *really* do, but when it happens I want it to be something we do because it's the right thing. Not because one of us wants to forget our problems for a while."

I closed my eyes, sucking in a deep breath. My body ached with the need to touch her, but I knew she was right.

I know with the way things are right now and with everything the two of you have gone through, it's tempting to jump into things because you think there might not be a tomorrow, Lake's words drifted through my head. *I just want you to really know what you're getting into before you act.*

I reached across the space between us, wrapping my arms around her waist and pulling her into a tight hug. Mara was tense at first, but then she relaxed, resting her head against my shoulder.

"I love you," Mara said.

It was the first time she had said the words to me, and a tingling warmth spread through my body.

"I love you too," I said, certain that I meant it.

Chapter 15

Dylan stepped out of his house just as I was passing by after leaving Mara's. He looked at me and nodded curtly, but didn't say anything.

We kind of fell into step next to each other, both of us keeping our heads down and our hands buried in our pockets. Not that my mind was on Dylan or even on my watch coming up at the beach. The threat of Domnall couldn't ruin the mood I was in right then. My mind was still stuck on that couch with Mara, reliving the feel of her body next to mine. Even though we hadn't made it as far as we might have, we still took advantage of the time alone to make out a lot.

I loved her. I could imagine myself spending my life with her.

I felt relaxed and at ease and in the best mood I'd been in months. So I thought it was a good time to try to make amends.

"Hey," I said, glancing at Dylan. "I'm sorry about yesterday."

Dylan harrumphed, then said, "What do you have to be sorry about?"

"I don't want to fight with you," I told him. "This isn't the time for us to be fighting with each other."

"Why does it matter?" Dylan asked. "You and I are not friends."

I tried to keep the cringe off my face at his words. "We could be. We both care about Mara and Sailor, so we should be friends."

Dylan sneered. "I'm not in desperate need of friends, you know. I've gotten along just fine without you."

He wasn't making this easy. He had always seemed like a nice guy, what little I knew of him from school. What had turned him into this negative, sour person?

"Whatever," I said, shrugging. "But for the record, the offer still stands if you change your mind."

We left his neighborhood and walked across Heron Avenue, following the sandy shoulder in front of the line of shops. I didn't ask where he was going, and he didn't ask me either.

The silence that had settled over us was broken by voices overhead as we neared Moody's Variety Store. The door closed behind Elizabeth Connors as she stepped out, with Kyle McCutcheon right behind her.

They spotted us as they walked down the staircase and Elizabeth's mouth twisted into a gleeful smile. She turned around to face Kyle, slipping her arms around his neck and leaning back to look up at him.

"Kiss me," she said.

Kyle's eyebrows shot up. "What?"

"Come on," she said in a syrupy voice. "You know you want me."

Kyle grinned, then leaned down, pressing his mouth to hers in a slobbering, sucking kiss that made my stomach turn. She was really laying the public displays of affection on pretty thick today.

"Let's go back to my house," Elizabeth said in a loud voice, glancing over her shoulder at us. "My parents should be gone for a while." She giggled and tightened her grip on Kyle's neck.

Dylan walked faster, not looking up at them. Good idea. I felt like I might puke if I had to listen to or see anymore of that. I quickened my pace and caught up with Dylan.

Once we had passed Moody's, Dylan muttered, "I don't know what the girls in this place see in jackasses like that."

I shrugged. "Some girls like jackasses, I guess."

"He's an oaf," Dylan growled. "He has no common sense. He treats girls like crap, and yet they still go back to him. Every time! It's ridiculous how stupid some people can be."

I peered at Dylan, furrowing my brow. "Why do you care?"

Dylan stumbled a bit as he walked, but he didn't look at me. "I don't. Elizabeth Connors can date whoever she wants. If she wants to throw herself all over an idiot, whatever. It's not my problem if all the jackasses on this island pair up. Let them have each other. I'm done with it."

Dylan turned off, stomping as he followed a narrow path between two sand dunes. I watched him for a moment, rolling his words over in my head and putting pieces together I hadn't noticed before.

I started walking again, considering the new idea that was forming in my head. It was crazy. It was too weird to even consider.

But it made sense. It would explain a lot of things. Dylan's bad attitude. Elizabeth's showing off.

Mara would probably say I was insane for even thinking it, but I was sure that something had happened while I was gone, something big, something that neither Dylan nor Elizabeth wanted anyone else to know.

* * *

I paced the stretch of beach, my eyes scanning the afternoon fog over the water. Nothing. There hadn't been anything since I'd started my shift three hours ago.

I wrapped my arms tighter around myself and stamped my feet on the sand, wishing I was back with Mara again right then and not out here on this freezing beach. Why was it so cold? It was mid-August for crying out loud.

A movement out of the corner of my eye made me spin around, my body tensed. But the figure that walked across the sand near the pier wasn't Domnall or any of his people. It wasn't even a finfolk at all.

It was my mom.

"Mom?" I asked as I approached her. I kept enough distance between us that hopefully she wouldn't become spooked and run off. Mom had never been well while I was growing up, always drifting in and out of weird spells that would make her yell or cry or throw things. She had been seeing a doctor on the mainland for years, but she never took her medicine regularly so it was hard to figure out what kind of mood she would be in from one moment to the next.

I hadn't seen her in days, not since she'd kicked me out. For the briefest moment, I thought that she had come to apologize and ask me to come home.

But the vacant look in Mom's eyes told me that she wasn't in one of her better moods.

Mom walked under the pier, weaving between the barnacle-covered pilings that held the remains of the rotting wood over our heads. The water crashed against the shore, lapping at my feet.

"Your daddy died here," she said. Her eyes were locked on the pier over us as she spoke.

I shivered. "You should go home."

"His body washed up on shore right over there." She pointed to a place just beyond the pilings, to a stretch of beach that looked like any other. No one ever talked much about my father, except that he had an affair and died because none of the finfolk in the water that night would save him. It was Song Night, and the water around Swans Landing was full of more finfolk than the number that currently lived here. But none of them had seen my father fall into the water.

He was buried in the cemetery near the white church on the island, but I had never known the exact spot where he'd died. Where he'd taken his last breaths. Where his body was found.

I stared at the beach Mom had indicated, trying to imagine him lying there, wet and covered with sand. Dead.

"The finfolk did that to him," Mom said, her eyes wide. "They've been an infestation on this island for centuries. They tried to pretend they were just like us. They fooled many of us many times. Your daddy fooled me for a while. Making me believe he was human. That those creatures meant nothing to him. But he was obsessed. All day and night, he'd be out here, watching and studying them. Talking to them. Trying to be one of them. And that girl, that whore he spent so much time with. It was disgusting."

She let out a loud bark of laughter, which echoed under the pier around us. "Oh, he denied it. He said she was just helping him. That she was a friend. But I could see it. We all could see the evidence right there, growing in her stomach, that bastard girl she gave birth to."

"Mom," I said, reaching toward her. "Go home. You should sleep. Have you taken your medicine today?"

But Mom swatted my hand away, twisting out of my reach. Her nostrils flared and her hair whipped around her head in a frenzy. "I did it for *you*, Joshua. All of it. I did it to protect you, to keep you from growing up with a daddy who didn't care enough not to destroy his family. I did it for you."

"What are you talking about?" I asked. "What did you do?"

Mom's eyes met mine, and I shuddered at the dark, glassy look in them. "You want to know how your daddy died, Joshua?" Her words roared in my ears over the sound of the crashing waves. Salt water sprayed across my skin as it hit the pilings around me.

"*I pushed him in*," Mom hissed.

I couldn't move, couldn't speak or think. My insides had turned to ice. A satisfied smile spread across Mom's face.

"He was here, up there." She pointed at the pier above us. "He was watching them. Watching *her*. Waiting for her to come back to him. There I was, at home with a baby while he was out here with his fish whore. So I followed him and I found him. He stood at the edge of the pier, on the part that's gone now. He didn't see me, didn't hear me coming. I pushed him off and watched him fall into the water. He hit his head on the pilings and—"

"No!" I stared at my mother, my entire body shaking so bad I almost couldn't stay upright. I reached out to steady myself against one of the pilings, then realized what I was touching. I stared at the wood, wondering if this was the one that had killed my father. Was this the one he'd hit, the one that had knocked him unconscious and made him unable to fight his way back to shore?

"I did it for you!" Mom shouted at me. She stepped forward, her arms reaching for me. "My baby. My little boy. I won't let them take you from me, like they did your daddy."

"Don't touch me." I backed away from her, staring at my mother. A trembling started deep inside my bones. My mom had killed my father. The man she was supposed to love. She had always told me it was the finfolk who did it. I had grown up fearing them, and then when I realized I was one of them, I had been afraid of that part of me. Afraid of what it was capable of making me do.

But it was the human part of me that I should have feared all along.

"Joshua—"

But Mom's words were cut off by a shout and a new sound from the water behind me.

Rising from the crashing waves was an army pulling a boat. A long, slender boat, in which stood Domnall, king of Hether Blether, his mouth twisted into a fierce snarl as his eyes met mine.

Chapter 16

Domnall stepped out of the boat, wading through knee high water until he stood on shore. The rest of the men and women that had come with him fanned out to each side. There were about twenty of them and they looked tired and thinner than before, their faces gaunt and cheekbones clearly visible.

But Domnall's smile was as wicked as I remembered. I moved in front of my mom, pushing her behind me.

"We meet again," Domnall said, inclining his head toward me in a mock bow.

"We're prepared for you," I told him. "We'll fight for this island."

"And the humans as well?" Domnall asked with a sneer. "Will you fight for them?"

"Filthy abominations!" Mom spat behind me. "Go back to the ocean where you belong!"

I tried to clamp a hand over her mouth, but Mom twisted away from me, screaming obscenities at the finfolk who stared evenly back at her, none of them seeming to be affected by her words. Artair, the captain of Domnall's guard, stood at his king's side, his face grim.

Domnall's eyes narrowed as he looked at Mom and then me. He opened his mouth and began to sing, a low humming that vibrated around us, mixing with the sound of the water.

Mom's cries fell silent as the first golden bursts sparkled in my vision. The human part of me made me susceptible to the song's effects, but Mom would be even more so, being fully human. Her eyes widened and her mouth dropped open in an O shape.

"Mom!" I called, squeezing my eyes shut. "Don't listen to it. It's not real. Whatever you see, it's not really there."

"Oliver!" Mom gasped. "I'm sorry. I'm so sorry!"

My body shook with the effort to resist the song that wrapped itself around me. I could feel the call of it inside me and still saw the golden bursts even with my eyes shut tight. "Josh," a voice whispered in my ear. A man's voice, one I had only ever imagined and couldn't be sure that it was right. I knew what I would see when I opened my eyes. I knew that it wasn't real, but yet, I couldn't stop myself from looking.

My father stood on the beach, smiling as he lifted a hand toward me. I bit my lip, choking back the sob in my throat. *It's not real,* I reminded myself.

But he looked so solid. Mom fell to her knees, her shoulders shaking. "Oliver," she said. "Forgive me."

"Their minds are so easily bent," Domnall said. The song started to fade as he stopped singing and I felt my own conscious mind coming back to me. "So weak. So foolish." He laughed. "Did you think I didn't know about your little secret? Your sister was careless in letting me find out that you had human blood."

I remembered when Sailor told me back in Hether Blether that Domnall suspected we were part human. He had sung, trying to get her to reveal the truth about herself, but she had resisted him. She had fought back.

We may have been human, but we were still finfolk too.

"Do you know that I can control her mind with the song?" Domnall asked. "What should I have her do? Drown herself?"

Mom stood on shaky legs and walked toward the ocean. She didn't notice when the cold water lapped at her knees. "Oliver," she gasped, pushing farther into the surf.

She had lied to me. She had killed my father and let me—let everyone—believe the finfolk had been to blame.

I clenched my jaw, fighting with myself. "No," I croaked out as I fought the effects of Domnall's song.

"No?" Domnall asked, and Mom dropped to her knees in the surf. Her body shook with sobs as she crawled back onto the sand.

"I didn't mean to, Oliver," she said, reaching a hand into the empty air, her eyes wide at the sight only she could see.

Murderer, a voice in my head whispered. But the person on her hands and knees in the sand didn't look like she could kill anyone. She cried out, her face wet with salt water and tears.

Domnall was singing again, louder this time. I had to get away from the song. They would come after me if I ran, still singing. There was only one way I could go to block out the sound. A way that wouldn't allow my mother to come with me. I had to make a choice. Stay and fall under their influence like my mother, or leave and save myself.

Mara. I had to save Mara. I had to warn everyone else that Domnall was here.

I squeezed my eyes shut, sucked in a deep breath, and then gritted my teeth as I opened my eyes again. I forced my foot to move. First one and then the other. I kept my gaze on the gray ocean, ignoring my mom's cries behind me.

"Stop him," Domnall growled, the song faltering as he spoke.

It was enough. I took the momentary relief to lunge forward, pushing myself across the sand and into the crashing waves.

My body tumbled through the current as the change overtook me. Pain seared through my bones as they popped and moved. My skin stretched and scales ripped through them, covering my legs as they fused into a tail fin.

They were sure to come after me. I knew that water couldn't stop them, but I had the element of surprise on my side, as well as the fact that I knew the island better than they did.

I launched myself through the water, staying under the surface to make it harder for them to track me. I swam as hard as I could, rocketing along the coast, following the curve of the land under the surface that I had swam hundreds of times. I knew how far it was from the pier at the northern end of the island to the next point, the halfway mark where someone else would be on patrol.

I barely paused during the change from finfolk to human, pushing myself toward the shore until my legs were two separate limbs again and I could walk. My jeans were tattered shreds, the ends floating around me on the water's surface.

The figure that waited on the beach had stood, his gaze focused on me as I rose from the water. I glanced over my shoulder, but there was no one else surfacing behind me. I hoped I had gotten ahead of them, I hoped I had bought us some time.

As I drew closer to shore, I could make out the long blonde hair that flapped in the wind and the tall, narrow body that tensed at my presence.

"Dylan!" I called as I pushed through the rolling surf that tried to pull me back out to sea. "They're here! The finfolk are here!"

Dylan's face lost all color and his scowl melted away. "Where?"

I pointed north. "Near the pier. They just surfaced. They have my mom."

Dylan raced across the sand without a word. I followed, climbing the dunes that separated the beach from the shops along this side of Heron Avenue. Dylan raced up the staircase that led to Moody's Variety Store while I sprinted across the street, turning corners until I reached the blue house up on stilts.

Bursting through the door, I called out as loud as I could, "They're here!"

Callum and Sailor appeared immediately, their faces both ghostly white. "Domnall?" Callum asked.

I nodded. "They came ashore near the pier. They're here."

"What do we do?" Sailor asked.

"You stay here," Callum told her. "I'll go. Maybe I can talk to them."

"I'm not staying behind!" Sailor exclaimed, shooting Callum a scowl. "If you go, I go."

I didn't have time to listen to them argue. I found my bag of clothes and peeled off the tattered jeans before pulling on a new pair. I understood now why the Hether Blether finfolk all wore robes.

I left the two of them arguing in the doorway while I raced back down the stairs. I cut through yards, jumping over fences and bushes and dodging dogs to reach Mara's house.

I pounded on her front door. "Mara! They're here!"

The door swung open, but it was Lake and not Mara who looked out at me. He looked like he hadn't slept at all in at least two days, and his face was covered with thick brown stubble.

"Where?" he asked calmly.

"The pier," I said.

Lake nodded, his face grim. He pushed past me and hurried down the stairs, running when he reached the ground.

"What's going on?" Mara appeared in the doorway, her eyes wide.

"They're here," I told her.

Her mouth dropped open. "We're out of time?"

I nodded. "And they have my mom."

Mara swallowed and then held her shoulders back. She stepped outside, reaching for my hand and entwining her fingers with mine. "Let's go," she said.

Chapter 17

The finfolk crested the dunes as we reached Heron Avenue. Lake, Mara, Dylan's parents, and I stood in a group on one side of the road. Behind them, another crowd approached. Dylan and Mr. Moody led the way with a few other finfolk and humans.

A jolt went through me when I saw my mother standing among Domnall's people. She looked even more lost and confused than usual, though no one was singing. What tricks did they know to create lasting effects on the human mind without the song?

Mara must have felt me tense, because she reached for my hand and squeezed tight.

"We do not wish to fight anyone," Domnall said, examining us and then the group behind him. He held his arms out, palms up, as if to show that he had no weapons. But he was dangerous even without being armed. "We have come in peace."

"Peace?" asked a voice behind me. I turned as Callum limped his way toward us, Sailor at his side. He stared at Domnall, his mouth curled into a snarl. "You've come to invade a land that doesn't belong to you. That is not my definition of peace."

"We have come," Domnall spoke in a louder voice, his shoulders back, "to reunite our people with those who are lost. We have come to strengthen the finfolk population, to offer you hope in a world controlled by humans."

"No, thanks," Lake said, crossing his arms. "We like our world the way it is."

"Only because you know nothing else," Domnall told him. "Your ancestors took away your chance to be with your own kind. They left their people behind, but we are offering you a choice. A chance to be whole, to be who you are meant to be, in a place where you are free to do it."

"And what exactly do you call freedom, Domnall?" Callum asked. He gestured at his leg, where the end of the metal leg stuck out from the bottom of his pants. "Cutting off limbs? That's your freedom? Restricting people to a single place? Instilling fear and hatred of the outside world?"

Domnall's eyes narrowed as he looked back at Callum. "You, dear brother, are a traitor to us. Your punishment is your own doing. As for the rest of your claims, everything I do is for the protection of my people. The human world has tainted us! It has introduced illness, of both mind and body. It has made us weak. United, we can be strong again. We can ensure that the race of our people continues for generations to come. That is what I offer you now. Hope. A future."

"And what about those of us who are human?" Mr. Richter asked. "Where do we fit into your new world?"

Domnall sneered. "Humans are of no concern to me."

Mr. Moody raised his shotgun, the barrel pointed steadily at Domnall. "There ain't no one here who wants your future, sir, so I suggest you get off our island."

Domnall turned to face Mr. Moody, looking unconcerned about the weapon pointed his way. He opened his mouth and the notes of the finfolk song filled the air. I clamped my hands over my ears, though it wouldn't block it out.

Mr. Moody's arms trembled and he blinked. He stared at something in front of him, lowering the gun. "Gale," he said, his voice trembling.

"That's enough!" Lake dashed forward, his face twisted in pain. He lunged at Domnall, but Artair and another guard stepped in his path, holding him back. It was enough to distract Domnall though, and the song faded, leaving Mr. Moody and the other humans shaking their heads.

"Very well," Domnall roared, his face red. "If you will not join us peacefully, we will find ways to convince you." He waved a hand toward Lake. "Take away his ability to change."

"No!" I shouted, stepping forward. Mara looked at me in confusion, but her eyes were wide. We hadn't explained one of the other things the finfolk could do with the song: use it to stop someone from changing to finfolk form. Domnall had had it done to Callum years ago. As he had explained to Sailor and me, it was a difficult process and took a lot of energy, a lot more than healing someone did. It was only done in extreme circumstances.

"You have no right, Domnall," Callum said through clenched teeth.

"I have every right," Domnall replied. "As I have reminded you before, you are not king, Callum. You gave up your claim."

He turned back to Artair. "Do it."

Artair looked at us and then at Domnall. He shifted from one foot to the other.

"Why do you hesitate?" Domnall snapped.

Artair took a deep breath. "I do not think—"

"You are not here to think! You are here to follow orders!"

Artair's hesitation gave Lake the opportunity to launch himself backward against the man, ramming his shoulder into Artair's chest. Artair stumbled backward, gasping. Other guards reached for Lake, but he ducked and twisted out of the way, racing toward us.

"Go!" he shouted. He grabbed Mara's arm, never pausing as he passed. I stumbled after them, my hand still clenched in hers. "Go!" Lake called over his shoulder. "Everyone, now!"

I didn't hesitate. I turned and ran, trying to keep up with Mara and Lake. Mara looked back at me just once, her eyes wide. She stumbled a bit over the sand, then turned back to run with her father.

Lake was fast, probably almost as fast as he could be in the water. He leaped over small brush as he raced down the street away from the beach and Domnall. I hadn't paid attention to everyone else, but I hoped they had managed to get away too.

Footsteps pounded on the asphalt behind me. I glanced over my shoulder just long enough to see that it was one of Domnall's men. Domnall must have ordered his guard to try to catch as many of us as they could. Wind roared in my ears as I ran, but I could hear the faint sound of the finfolk song. My feet moved on their own, slowing just slightly. Gold sparks burst at the edges of my vision.

"Josh! Keep running!"

I blinked, shaking my head. Mara's voice brought me back from the haze that had settled over my mind. She and Lake were getting farther away, but still close enough that the guard behind me might be able to catch them.

He couldn't find out where they were going. I couldn't let Domnall know where to look for Mara.

I veered off to the right, dashing in between shops. Just as I'd hoped, the guard turned too, following me. It was a very risky move, giving him the chance to get me alone, but at least Mara could get away.

I dodged between shops and then homes, jumping over bushes and a kid's red wagon. The guard was still a few feet behind me, but I had the advantage. I had grown up in Swans Landing, and I knew every inch of it.

Gritting my teeth, I pushed myself harder. I had to get ahead enough to hide. The shops and homes along Heron Avenue changed into open grassland and dunes the farther north I ran. I could see the black and white lighthouse rising ahead and then the ferry dock near it. There was no ferry docked in the harbor, since it hadn't come at all that day.

I reached the fence that marked the parking lot of the harbor with still a good distance between myself and the finfolk guard. I glanced back just long enough to see how much time I had. Seconds, maybe, if I was lucky.

I dashed across the gravel parking lot toward the dock. Jumping over the metal bars that served as a gate, I ran to the edge of the wooden dock and then jumped into the water, as quickly and fluidly as I could. It occurred to me as I sank below the surface that I was ruining yet another pair of jeans.

The change took over me and I fell deep below the surface, trying not to thrash too much or let out any air bubbles that would let the guard know where I was. He could change too, so he could jump in after me if he wanted, but I hoped that maybe he would go back to Domnall instead.

Once my change was done, I didn't dare go near the surface. Instead, I stayed as close to the sandy bottom as I could. I floated just inches above the sand, not daring to move even an inch for a long time. I didn't know how much time passed, but it felt like an eternity. Every fish that swam my way made my heart lurch, certain that it was the finfolk guard coming after me.

But the water remained still and I was alone. When I felt brave enough, I slowly swam west toward the sound side of the island. I paused long enough to study the murky water around me, but there was no sign that anyone else was following.

Finally, I let out the breath I'd been holding.

* * *

"Any luck?" Lake asked as Mr. Richter sat down at the island counter in Miss Gale's kitchen.

Mr. Richter sighed. "I've called as many people as I could reach. Most of them didn't seem too worried about my warnings. Harry Connors hung up on me."

Lake rubbed a hand over his face, sighing. "I don't know what else we can do. We're trying to help and they won't even listen to us."

Mara and I exchanged a worried look. There weren't many year round residents of Swans Landing, a few hundred, but there were enough that the people who weren't here with us could have been in more danger than they realized. I had made my way to the sound side of the island an hour ago and came ashore near Miss Gale's house. The finfolk guard who had followed me to the ferry dock was nowhere to be seen, but I still had raced for safety as quickly as I could.

A small crowd had gathered at Miss Gale's. We had taped up all the windows in the house, covering them with black trash bags and blankets, and stuffed towels against all the doors that led outside, trying to block out any sounds, any bit of song that the finfolk out there might try to use to lure us out. Mara had already called her friend Claire and warned her to keep her doors locked and her family inside. I hoped that maybe the rest of the humans on the island would make it through the night.

I slid my glass of salt water across the counter, staring at the liquid inside. Domnall had my mom. I hated to think what he might be doing to her.

But a part of me—a small, tiny part—wondered if I should leave her to her fate with the finfolk. *She killed my father*. She had lied to me, let me believe that someone else was responsible for his death. But it had been her. She had always known the truth.

And yet, she was my mother. There was a kind, sensitive woman somewhere inside her. I had glimpsed it a few times throughout my life, when she would bandage up my scrapes and sing me to sleep.

111

"So what's the plan?" Mara asked. "How do we defeat them?"

"We can't," Callum said. He sat on the couch behind us, with Sailor at his side. Dylan leaned against the refrigerator, avoiding looking at them.

"What?" Mr. Moody asked in his low growl.

"They know more than you do," Callum said. "They know how to use the songs in ways that the finfolk here don't." He looked at Mara, Lake, Dylan, and then me. "You're also part human, and that makes you weak."

"But aren't they part human too?" I asked. "You said some of the finfolk in Hether Blether had human blood."

Callum nodded. "Right. But Domnall would know not to bring along people that have weakened blood. He wouldn't want his guard to be susceptible to the song's influence like humans are. So the people he brought with him are most likely all pure finfolk. None of them reacted to the song, did they?"

The rest of us exchanged uneasy looks. Domnall's group was small, no more than twenty men and women, but if they could use the songs against us, we didn't have much of a chance.

"There has to be a way," I said.

"Unless you can turn all of you into full-blooded finfolk, there isn't," Callum said. "You'll be vulnerable to even the weakest finfolk song with your human blood."

There were some finfolk in Swans Landing who had so little human blood in them that they considered themselves fully finfolk. People like Miss Gale, whose last human ancestor was many generations before her. But still, she had the human genes and she was vulnerable to the song's effects too. We all were.

"The key."

Our heads snapped toward the hall where Coral stood. Her white nightgown fluttered around her feet and her skin was as pale as the cloth, making her look like a ghost. She twisted her fingers around each other as she took another step into the room.

"Coral," Lake said gently, "you should go to sleep."

But Coral didn't look at him. She stared at me, her blue eyes wide. "The key," she said again, in a whisper. Frantic lines formed between her eyes. "You have to use the key. Remember?"

I shook my head. "I don't know what you mean. What about the key? What did my dad tell you?"

But she looked agitated and turned, pacing the room in her bare feet. "It's the only way," she said to herself. "I brought it back, just like he told me to. He knows what to do."

Sailor stood and rushed to her mother's side, slipping her arm around her shoulders. "It's okay, Mama," Sailor said. She ran a hand over her mother's hair and led her back into the hall.

The rest of us sat silently after they'd left. Mr. Moody cleared his throat, then he rose from his seat and disappeared into the hall after them.

* * *

I rolled the finfolk key over in my hands, rubbing my thumb across the rough surface. I bounced it between one hand and the other, inspecting every part of the twisted metal.

But it didn't tell me anything I didn't know before. If my dad had told Coral something about this key, it wasn't anything obvious. *I need answers, Dad,* I thought. *Tell me something.*

"Hey." Mara sat down next to me on the floor where I had set up my makeshift bed. With so many people now staying at the Mooring house, I had given up the couch to Mr. Moody. But it didn't seem like anyone would be getting much sleep that night. The adults were all still up, keeping watch from the tiny attic window. Dylan's little brother Reed was passed out on the love seat while everyone else was scattered throughout the house.

"Hey," I greeted her.

Mara snuggled close to me, slipping her arm through mine. "Figured anything out?"

I shook my head. "I don't know what I'm supposed to do with this."

"Is there anything in your dad's papers?" Mara asked.

"Not that I've found yet." I motioned to the stack in my lap. "I still have a lot of reading to do."

I sighed and closed my eyes, leaning my head back against the wall behind me. I was tired, but it was more of a mental fatigue than physical. My body felt too wired and jumpy for sleep.

"You okay?" Mara asked.

I opened my eyes, surveying the room. We were alone, as alone as we could be in a crowded house. No one was close enough to overhear us if we talked quietly.

"Something happened right before the finfolk showed up," I said. I looked down at my clenched hands on top of the notebook in my lap. "My mom told me something about the night my dad died."

"What is it?" Mara asked gently.

I sucked in a shaking breath. "She said she followed him to the pier that night. All the finfolk were in the water because it was song night. She saw him there, waiting for Coral to join him. My mom..." I paused, the words getting stuck in my throat. I swallowed and tried again. "My mom pushed my dad off the pier."

"Your mom..." Mara left the sentence unfinished, her face twisted into disbelief.

I nodded. "*My mom* killed my dad. You've heard what people have said. The water was rough that night, too rough for a human. He hit the pilings and drowned. His body washed up onshore the next morning."

"But why?" Mara asked, pressing herself closer to me. "Why should she do that?"

"She said it was to protect me," I told her. "To keep me from growing up with a father who chose to leave his family. But I don't know what to believe anymore. All this time, I thought that the finfolk part of me was the dangerous part, the one I should be afraid of. But maybe the human part is the cruelest. Maybe that's the one I should fear."

"You're not your parents, Josh," Mara said. "What they did doesn't make you a bad person. Being finfolk or human doesn't make you evil. One isn't better than the other. They're both you."

"I'm not sure that being me is a good thing."

Mara pushed the papers off my lap and positioned herself on my legs, her face close to mine. "Being you is a great thing," she said. "Don't forget that."

Her lips were soft and warm, and I closed my eyes, reveling in the feel of them. I hugged her close, not wanting to let go.

A cough made us break apart and heat crept up my neck when I saw Lake watching us from across the room.

"It's getting late," he said. "Mara, you can share Sailor's room."

Mara rolled her eyes as she stood. "It'll be just like a slumber party."

She gave me a small wave as she disappeared into the hall, leaving me still facing Lake. He narrowed his eyes at me, his arms crossed. I rubbed the back of my neck, avoiding his gaze though I could still feel it on my skin. He knew I'd almost had sex with his daughter. He had to know, or at least suspect. He had that pissed off dad look.

Finally, when I felt like my head was about to explode, Lake turned away, leaving me still twitching on the floor.

Chapter 18

I couldn't sleep. I had been lying on my makeshift bed on the floor of the living room for hours, but my mind wouldn't stop thinking over all of the events of that day.

Domnall was here and he had my mom.

My mom, who had killed my father. My father, who'd had an affair and another child. Both sides of my parentage were tainted.

The room felt stuffy. Dylan slept on a blanket only two feet away, his brother snoring next to him. Mrs. Waverly was on the couch, trying to get a few hours of sleep before she would go up to take over the watch in the attic. Callum slept on the love seat, his arms over his head.

I tiptoed across the room to the back door, sliding it open as quietly as I could. Cool night air drifted toward me, prickling my skin. The sky was dark, thick with fog, and the island was silent. Even the constant swish of the ocean a few blocks away sounded muted, like it too was trying to be quieter.

I needed some air and some solitude. Closing the door behind me, I slipped across the wooden deck and down the stairs to the backyard. The small attic window was only on one side of the house, so I didn't think I could be seen, and the darkness helped give me more cover.

I stood in the grass, sucking the salt air deep into my lungs. Somewhere out there, the finfolk had my mom. What were they doing to her?

My feet started moving before I realized I was leaving the Mooring yard. I slipped between houses and along the shriveled shrubbery, my senses on high alert for any sign of movement. I strained my ears to hear even the slightest sound of a song, but there was nothing except the ocean in the background.

I hesitated when I reached Moody's Variety Store, pausing in the shadows. I should go back to Miss Gale's house and go to sleep. If anyone noticed I was gone, I would be in major trouble. If the finfolk found me, I would be in even more trouble.

I didn't want to see my mom, but I wanted to know what Domnall was doing to the humans. Shrubbery shivered to my my left and I jumped, my muscles tensed, legs ready to spring into a run. I had no weapons to help me fight off the finfolk, but I would run as fast I could and hope that it would be enough. I grit my teeth, searching the shadows for danger.

But the creature that emerged from the brush was a small gray cat. It caught sight of me, sniffing the air for only a brief moment before darting back toward safety.

I let out a long breath, closing my eyes as my shoulders sagged.

I kept moving through the night, creeping closer to the beach. The clouds overhead blocked out most of the moonlight, so the night was almost black.

The voices reached me before I spotted the two figures standing by the dunes.

"They are all asleep," Artair's voice drifted toward me. "We could surprise them now."

"Do you think I care much about the people, Artair?" Domnall asked, his voice sounding tired and weary. "They are only obstacles that can be easily removed when they get in my way. Has everyone returned from their searches?"

"Yes, my king," Artair answered. "The others have searched the waters, but they have not found it yet." He paused, then said, "Maybe it is not here."

"It is here," Domnall said. "I know it is. The finfolk here do not even realize what they have opened."

"Yes, my king."

The dark figure took a few steps forward along the sand dune, the wind whipping his long hair back from his shoulders. I recognized Domnall's wide form.

"Sing to me, Artair," Domnall said.

"My king?" Artair asked.

"Just for a moment. I want to see her."

"Yes, my king," Artair said.

I backed up quickly, my feet slipping over the sand. I had to get far enough away that I wouldn't hear the song while Artair sang. I couldn't risk falling under the spell and letting them find me.

In the safety of the darkness under Moody's Variety Store, I pressed my hands to my ears and squeezed my eyes shut. I stood like that for a long time, praying for the strength to resist the song's effects.

After what seemed like an eternity, I dared to remove my hands from my ears and listened hard. All I could hear was the constant roar of the ocean. My body relaxed as I let out a long sigh.

"You are brave, coming out here alone," said a low voice behind me. Something sharp pierced the skin of my back and I fought not to move at the pain. "Or else incredibly stupid."

I turned around slowly, my hands held up like I was being arrested. Artair stood in the shadows behind me, a knife in his hand. It looked strange to see him with such a smaller weapon than the spear he had always carried back in Hether Blether, but I guessed the larger weapon didn't make the journey across the ocean. The knife was a black handled steak knife, probably something he had found in a human's home or in a store on the island. My stomach churned as I thought about how many other humans the finfolk might have captured that day.

"Where's my mother?" I asked.

He studied me, keeping the knife pointed toward me. "The woman you were with this morning on the beach? She is fine. She is being kept with the others."

I gulped. "How many humans do you have?"

Artair shrugged. "A few. Most have stayed hidden in their homes, but they cannot hide forever. Domnall will draw them out."

His hand stayed steady, the tip of the knife still directed toward my stomach, but his face didn't hold his usual stern expression. I thought about how he had hesitated on the beach when Domnall had told him to take away Lake's ability to change.

"You don't have to do this," I told him. "You don't have to follow Domnall's orders."

"He is my king," Artair said, his voice flat.

"Whenever any form of government becomes destructive of these ends, it is the right of the people to alter or to abolish it," I recited.

Artair blinked at me, his face blank.

"Those are the words of my people," I said. "The Declaration of Independence, written by *humans*. If your king is not acting for the good of your people, you can demand a new one."

Artair sneered. "We are not human. We are finfolk, and we live by our own laws." He lifted the knife higher, aiming it at my neck. "I should take you to Domnall now. He would be happy to have captured you."

"You're not like that." I stared back at him, clenching my fists to keep my hands from shaking. "You are different."

Artair's face turned red, the color sweeping down his neck. "No, I am not! Do not ever say that again. I am finfolk, all the way through." His eyes flashed, like I had hit a nerve.

I thought about what I knew of Artair. He was Domnall's guard, seemingly the equivalent of a captain and Domnall's most trusted man. Sailor and I had seen him with his family in Hether Blether, in the village market and at the beach. He had a wife and a young daughter.

"You are different," I said. "You're a father. How can you tear families apart just because they're human? You have my mother. How would your daughter feel if someone did this to you?"

Artair's face paled. He leaned toward me, his teeth clenched. "Do not speak of my daughter." But his hand trembled, the knife shaking a little.

"What Domnall is doing is wrong," I insisted. "You know that. How can you let him use the song to control people? It's not right." I could never imagine myself manipulating people that way. The thought of using the song to make people do things against their will filled my mouth with a sour taste.

He took a step back and then lowered his weapon. He turned away from me and said, "You have only a moment before I change my mind and alert Domnall to your presence. Go."

I turned, intending to run, but then I looked back at the man standing in the shadows.

"Why is Domnall so insistent on taking the island?" I asked. "Why can't he just take whatever finfolk want to go to Hether Blether back with him and leave us in peace?"

Artair considered me a moment, then he said, "It is not the finfolk that Domnall came here for. He is looking for something that he believes now exists here on your island."

"What?" I asked.

"The door to Finfolkaheem."

The finfolk underwater homeland? That didn't make sense. The door had been in Hether Blether once, Callum had told us that, but it had closed long ago. Swans Landing didn't have the connection to the ancient city that Hether Blether did.

I shook my head. "The door isn't here."

Artair raised his eyebrows. "Are you certain about that?" Then he turned and stepped into the darkness.

Chapter 19

After my encounter with Artair, I made it back to Miss Gale's house unseen. I'd crawled back into my bed on the floor, but sleep wouldn't come. I tossed and turned most of the night, thinking about what Artair had told me. Domnall thought that the door to Finfolkaheem, the ancient underwater city, was here. If it was, where was it?

If the door was here in Swans Landing now, I had to find it before Domnall did. I had to reach the finfolk there and convince them to help us.

The mood in the house was quiet and somber most of the morning. Lake and the other adults met together in the kitchen, trying to come up with a plan for driving Domnall away.

"You can't fight them," Callum said. "You're weak."

"Maybe we should resort to other weapons," Mr. Moody said, glancing at the old shotgun he'd leaned against the wall.

But Callum sighed and shook his head. "You're not listening. Domnall will manipulate your mind before you even get a chance to fire at him. Humans aren't any trouble for him, and the finfolk on this island are only slightly less weakened."

Lake leaned over the island counter, his hands, calloused and cracked from years of work on the water, clasped together. "So what is our option? What can we do?"

"Nothing," Callum said. "Hide here and hope that Domnall doesn't decide to come in after you."

Mr. Richter ran a hand through his thick hair. "We can't sit here forever. We'll run out of food eventually. And there are others on the island. We have no idea what's happening with them."

"I've tried to call as many people as I could," Mr. Waverly said. "A lot of them aren't answering their phones."

Mara, Sailor, Dylan, and I sat in the living room, trying not to be noticed by the others as they talked. I wanted to be a part of their planning, but it was clear that they didn't consider us anything more than kids. I stayed still and quiet, hoping to hear something useful. I didn't dare tell them about my trip out to the beach the night before or how Artair had caught me. Which meant that I also couldn't tell them that I knew what Domnall wanted to find.

"We need to check on the others on the island," Lake said. "To find out how many are still able to fight against the finfolk, and how many are willing."

Callum stood. "I will go," he said. "I'll check on as many people as I can."

"No," Sailor said as she leaped up from the couch.

Lake hesitated, then he said, "I don't know if it's a good idea."

"I am the best option you have," Callum pointed out. "I'm fully finfolk, so I'm not susceptible to the song like the rest of you."

The others exchanged a look.

"He's right," Mr. Moody said. "He's our only option."

Lake nodded. "I can't tell you not to go, Callum. The choice is yours. But no one else can go with you."

Sailor wrapped her arms around Callum, burying her face in his chest. "Don't go," she said.

Callum kissed the top of her head. "I'll be fine. I've dealt with Domnall before."

"And he cut off your leg! I don't want to lose you."

"You won't," he assured her. "I'll be back before you know it. We'll end this. We'll find a way."

But he didn't sound any more confident than I felt.

Callum and Sailor said their good-byes and then Callum slipped out the door, with instructions from Lake and Mr. Richter on which homes to make sure he visited. Mr. Moody peeked through the curtain over one of the windows, watching as Callum disappeared.

"Are we sure we can trust him?" Mr. Moody asked.

"Of course we can," Sailor snapped.

Mr. Moody turned from the window and gave her a weary look. "I know you care about him, but he is still one of them. We have to be careful about who we trust."

"We can trust him." Sailor crossed her arms and looked at me. "Right, Josh?"

I nodded. "He's never given us any reason not to trust him."

We all went back to what we had been doing before while we waited for Callum's return, which for me meant reading some of my dad's papers. Morning stretched into afternoon, and then afternoon toward evening. And still, there was no sign of Callum.

Sailor peeked out of the curtain at the darkened street. "Something's happened," she said.

"Something happened all right," Dylan muttered. "He went back to his own kind. I told you we couldn't trust him."

Sailor whirled around to face him, her nostrils flared and her cheeks red. "Callum is not one of them!" she shouted. "He's on our side. When are you going to accept that?"

"Then where is he now?" Dylan asked.

"Domnall must have caught him," Sailor said. "He probably needs our help. We need to go after him."

"No," Lake said, standing from the barstool at the counter where he had been eating a box of cheese flavored crackers. "No one is leaving this house."

Sailor's eyes shone with tears. "But he could be in trouble. We *have* to help him."

"Or he could be with Domnall, working with him," Lake said grimly. "We don't know, and we can't risk it right now."

Sailor's body trembled and her face turned so dark, she looked like she might explode at any moment. I put my hand on her shoulder.

"Callum isn't working with Domnall," I said.

"How do you know?" Dylan asked.

Mara scowled at him. "Dylan, stop. If Josh and Sailor believe that Callum is on our side, that should be good enough for all of us."

Dylan crossed his arms. "None of you are willing to face the fact that you don't know this guy as well as you think. If you don't wake up soon, you're going to get us all killed."

I didn't want to believe that Callum might have joined Domnall. But without knowing the truth about what had happened to Callum that day, even I couldn't argue forever for his innocence. And if he was really on our side, then what had happened to him? I didn't want to think about what Domnall might have done if he had caught Callum.

"We can't do anything about it right now," Lake said. "It's too dangerous to go out in the dark, when they could be hiding anywhere, waiting for us. They have the advantage right now of already being out there. In the morning, if Callum still isn't back, some of us will go to try to find him."

Mr. Moody nodded. "That's all that we can do for now, I reckon."

"Let's all just get some sleep," Lake said.

But sleep felt like something that would never come.

Chapter 20

I woke with a start, my muscles tensed. I lay quietly on my blanket in the corner, staring up at the skylights overhead, my heart still pounding against my ribs.

For a moment, I thought I had heard the song. I thought my dad was there, his hand stretched toward me. His lips were moving, but I couldn't hear his voice over the humming in my ears. Then my mom screamed and I woke up.

A dream. Just a dream.

A sound startled me and I lifted my head, blinking as I looked across the room. Dylan was in the kitchen, opening cabinets.

"Didn't mean to wake you," he said when I slid into a barstool at the counter.

I rubbed my eyes and looked at the clock over the stove. 6:17 A.M. The last time I had remembered looking at the time, it was nearly four. I had managed a couple hours of sleep at least.

Dylan's eyes were ringed with dark circles. He didn't look like he'd gotten any more sleep than I had.

"Is everyone else still sleeping?" I asked quietly. His brother's snores drifted to us from the couch. I only knew

Reed vaguely, in the way that everyone in Swans Landing knew everyone else. He was twelve, so our paths didn't cross much.

Dylan nodded. "I think Lake and my parents and the others are still up in the attic, taking shifts at keeping watch. I saw Mr. Moody down here a little while ago, checking the doors. Then he went back up."

"How long have you been up?" I asked.

"An hour or so," Dylan said, shrugging. He found a box of granola bars and offered me one. I took it, tearing the wrapper quietly. Salty peanut flavor, I noted. Finfolk loved their salt.

We chewed our granola bars in silence. I could hear the soft tone of muffled voices floating down from the attic over this part of the house, but I couldn't make out the words.

I thought of my mother, wondering how she was doing and what might be happening to her.

"Do you think everyone else is okay?" Dylan asked, as if he had sensed my thoughts.

I rubbed a hand over my head, scratching at my scalp. "I don't know. I hope so. But I don't know."

Dylan tapped his fingers on the countertop, biting his lip.

"We need to get more people to work with us," I said. "There are more of us Swansers than there are of them. Maybe we could take them by surprise, overpower them or something."

"The humans won't work with us," Dylan said.

"Then you have to convince them."

Dylan rolled his eyes. "Sure, let me get right on that. And they'll listen to me because…?"

"Maybe they all won't listen to you," I said. "But Elizabeth will."

Dylan's gaze darted toward me, his nostrils flared. "What makes you think that?"

"Because I know that something happened between you and Elizabeth," I said. "Recently, I would guess. While Sailor and I were gone."

"You're insane." Dylan turned toward the sink and grabbed a glass, filling it with water.

"I'm observant," I corrected him. "I see the way the two of you look at each other. How mad you got yesterday when Elizabeth was all over Kyle. She shows off just to piss you off. The two of you can't help talking about each other, insisting that you don't really care."

Dylan spun around, his fingers gripping the glass. "I don't know what you're talking about, Canavan."

"Cut the crap, Waverly. I don't care about the details of your sex life or whether you even have one, but this is more important than that. You have to talk to Elizabeth and you have to get her to listen to you. If you don't want her to get hurt, you have to talk to her."

"Elizabeth Connors is not my problem," Dylan growled.

"If you don't do something to help her, then you're not the caring guy I always thought you were."

Dylan glared at me, then snatched up the salt shaker and dumped salt into his water. He drank it down, gulping the water and sighing when he was done. He wiped his mouth with the back of his hand and then set the glass in the sink.

"Fine," he said. "I'll talk to her."

* * *

We tried calling Elizabeth and texting her, but she wouldn't answer either one. Dylan looked up at me, his hair hanging in his face as he leaned over the island countertop, and I could see the worry in his eyes.

"Do you think they already got to her?" he asked.

I pressed my lips together, not wanting him to see the anxiety that I felt growing inside me. I couldn't guarantee anything at the moment with Domnall and his people on the island.

"We'll have to go to her," I said.

Dylan's eyebrows shot up. "What if the finfolk are out there waiting for us?"

"Do we really have a choice?" I asked. "Either we hide out in here until we run out of food, or we go out and try to save as many people as we can."

We decided not to wake anyone or let them know that we were leaving. I was sure they'd try to stop us, after Callum's disappearance. I didn't want to worry Mara or Dylan's parents. We'd go out, talk to Elizabeth, and then come back. We'd be careful. The residential area of Swans Landing wasn't very big, and so Elizabeth's house wasn't far from Sailor's. We could sneak through yards and use the other houses in between as cover. We had an advantage over Callum, being native Swansers and knowing the island like the back of our hands.

Besides, Artair had already let me go once. I was sure I could convince him to overlook me again. He wasn't like Domnall, no matter what he said.

I closed the door as quietly as I could and then the two of us slipped down the stairs, ducking as we rounded the side of the house to avoid being seen from the small attic window. It wasn't much of a lookout, since it was tiny and was never meant to provide a view. Hopefully the angle from the window wasn't good enough to let the people up there see us.

Of course, that also meant that they would never see the finfolk if they came up on that side of the house.

The island was quiet that morning. Too quiet. Goosebumps prickled all along my arms as we ran half-crouched past the house behind the Mooring home. We ducked behind a large rhododendron, peering out to look for signs of anyone else. There was nothing. Not even birds swooping overhead.

"Does it feel like everything has disappeared to you, or is it just me?" Dylan muttered next to me.

I nodded. "It feels wrong. Too still."

I didn't know what that meant for the rest of the population of Swans Landing. The finfolk who weren't with us at Miss Gale's house had been called and warned last night to stay in their homes. But there were still the humans who weren't on our side, who had refused to listen to our warnings.

Dylan shifted, snapping a twig under his foot. I jumped at the noise.

"Sorry," he whispered.

We raced away from our hiding place, hurrying across the narrow street to the next yard. My gaze darted from one side to the other as we slipped between houses and over fences. My body was so tense, I didn't realize I was clenching my jaw until it started to ache.

Finally, we reached the sea foam green house where Elizabeth lived. We ducked under the house, hiding behind a black car that didn't look as if it had been used in a long time. Most people didn't drive their cars around the island, saving them for trips on the ferry to the mainland.

"Should we ring the doorbell?" I asked.

Dylan snorted. "And have her dad slam it in our faces? Yeah, that'll work great."

"Text her," I said. "See if you can get her to let us in."

"I have a better idea." Dylan grabbed a ladder that hung from two hooks above us and carried it around the side of the house. He leaned it against the wooden deck that wrapped around most of the house, then he climbed up.

"I know which room is hers," Dylan told me.

I smirked. "I'll bet you do."

I glanced around, scanning the area, but we were still alone, so I climbed up after him. We crawled on our knees to the edge of the deck, where a single window hung just past the edge of the railing.

Dylan got up on his knees and tapped on the window. We waited, shivering in the cool morning air, but there was no response. Dylan tapped again, harder and longer.

The curtains over the window shifted and Elizabeth peered out at us, her hair tousled and her eyes only half-open. Shock passed across her face when she spotted us, quickly replaced by a scowl.

The window slid open and Elizabeth leaned out. "What the hell?" she whispered. "Do you two have any idea what time it is?"

"You need to listen to us," Dylan told her. "There are people here who are very dangerous. They'll come after you and your family."

Elizabeth crossed her arms. She wore a thin cotton T-shirt, which was slightly transparent. I fought hard to keep my gaze on her face.

"Is this about all that crap Mr. Richter was calling about last night? My daddy said he's as crazy as the rest of you fish people."

"This is serious," I said. "These people have come for us finfolk. They don't care about you, and they won't be nice if you get in their way."

She sneered. "I don't plan to get in their way. If they want you freaks, they can have you." Her eyes moved toward Dylan, her expression hardening. "*All* of you."

"Elizabeth," Dylan said, "this is not a game—"

"Go back to the ocean, Fish Boy." Then she slammed the window shut, pulling the curtains tight.

"Dammit," Dylan muttered. He raised a fist like he was going to punch through the glass and make her listen, but then he lowered his hand. "Fine. If that's the way she wants to be, she's on her own."

He crawled to the ladder and made his way down. I eased myself over the edge and climbed back to the ground, pulling the ladder down and tossing it into the grass.

"Why don't you just tell her you still like her?" I asked.

Dylan's eyes narrowed. "Because I don't."

"Like hell you don't. Look at how tense and wound up you are. If I hadn't been there, you'd probably have crawled right into her window. Maybe if you had, she would have listened to you."

"I don't give a damn about Elizabeth Connors," Dylan told me through clenched teeth.

"Does anyone else know about you and her?" I asked. "Does Mara know?"

Dylan spun around and stalked across the yard, his fists clenched.

"So what happened?" I asked, hurrying to catch up to him. "Whose idea was it? It had to be hers, right? So Elizabeth threw herself at you, you took advantage of the action, and then what? You threatened to tell everyone? You wanted her to be your girlfriend? Or did she figure out she was just a replacement because you couldn't have Mara?"

Dylan whirled around, moving too fast for me to react. His fist connected with the side of my face, my teeth ripping into my gums on the impact. I spit out a mouthful of blood, wiping my chin with the back of my hand.

Dylan looked as surprised as I felt, his eyes wide as he stared at me. Fury surged through me, starting in my toes and racing up my body. I hated him for how easy he'd had it. What had he done these last five months? He stayed in Swans Landing while Sailor and I swam four thousands miles each way. He got to spend five months with Mara that I hadn't had. He'd apparently spent time running around the island with Elizabeth, and I had a pretty good idea of what he might have been doing in her bedroom.

He'd never had to lie about who he was. His mother hadn't killed his father. He had nothing to complain about and all he'd done since I'd gotten back was whine and moan. I was sick of it.

I lunged, pushing him backward into the street. His head hit the asphalt and he groaned, but he was pushing back at me within seconds. We rolled over each other, arms swinging. Pain seared across my face when his fist hit my left eye and then he gasped when I punched him in the gut.

It felt good. All of the frustration I'd been holding inside for too long was coming out of me as I pummeled Dylan. I wanted to beat him until there was nothing left.

Gold bursts sparked in front of my eyes and my swing wavered, missing Dylan's ear. Through the haze that had begun to settle over me, I saw him shaking his head and blinking.

I became aware of a new sound that had broken the silence around us: the finfolk song.

Domnall and his guards stood only a few feet away, watching us as Domnall sang.

I rolled off Dylan, pressing my hands over my ears. "Don't look at it," I said. "Fight it."

Dylan groaned next to me. My body shuddered as I fought against the urge to follow the song. That was the most dangerous part of it. Not that it showed me what I wanted, but that it would make me follow it straight to Domnall.

We had to get away. I rolled over, bracing myself on my knees and elbows, trying to push myself up from the asphalt. "Dylan," I croaked. "Get up. We have to run."

"Joshua," a voice said, the sound drifting on the wind toward me.

I shuddered. I wouldn't look. It wasn't really my dad. He was dead. He was never coming back.

"Joshua," the voice said again.

No! It wasn't him. It couldn't be him, I knew that.

"I'm here, Joshua," the voice said.

I couldn't help it. Even as my eyelids slid open, the voice in my head yelled at me not to do it, to keep my eyes closed and run as hard as I could.

But I was human and I was weak.

Chapter 21

"Dad," I gasped, reaching out toward him. He stood there, solid and real, his hand stretched toward me, beckoning. Small rocks and broken shells dug into my palms as I crawled forward.

"Joshua," my dad said, smiling. "Come here."

"Dad!" Tears stung my eyes and I crawled faster, stumbling as a rock stabbed painfully into my knee.

But then another voice shattered my focus on the vision of my dad. "*No!*" Through the haze that had filled my mind I saw Elizabeth race across the grass, still dressed in her thin T-shirt, flat ankle boots on her feet. She moved in front of Dylan, her arms spread as she glared at Domnall. "Get away from them!"

Only Artair's face changed as he looked at Elizabeth, standing defiantly in front of the group. He shifted, his gaze darting to Domnall briefly, before his face took on his usual detached, stern look.

Domnall didn't seem bothered by Elizabeth's arrival. He continued to sing, his eyes locked on her, the corners of his lips curled into a smile.

"No," Elizabeth said, but I could see the way her body shook. I squeezed my eyes shut, telling myself not to look again. I turned around, the movements slow and painful as I resisted the call of the song that surged through me.

I followed the sound of Elizabeth's choked sob, not daring to open my eyes. "Dylan," she said, her voice breaking.

"It's not real, Elizabeth," Dylan said, his own voice strained. "Fight it."

But she didn't have the advantage of finfolk blood. She would be even more vulnerable to the song's effects. I reached out, my hand swiping at empty air. If I could find her, even just her leg, I could try to hold her back.

The crack of a gun's discharge exploded through the neighborhood. My eyelids snapped open wide to find the source of the sound.

Mr. Connors stood at the edge of the yard, his silver handgun clutched in one hand. "That was a warning shot," he boomed, his focus on the finfolk. "You touch my daughter and the next one will be in your head."

Domnall had stopped singing at the sound of the gun, but now he turned toward the other man, his face twisted into a wicked snarl. "You have no power here, human," he said. "Your little weapons are useless."

Mr. Connors raised the gun, aiming at the finfolk king, but Domnall began to sing again, louder this time. The song roared through the air, the notes hungry and furious. Mr. Connors let the gun fall to the ground and he took a step forward.

"C—" His mouth opened and closed as he tried to form words, his eyes wide and glassy.

"Josh!" Dylan rose from his place on the street, staggering forward. "Get up! Run!"

He darted forward, grabbing Elizabeth by the arm and dragging her behind him. I forced myself up onto unsteady legs, stumbling as I told myself not to look at the golden bursts where I knew my dad would appear.

As I regained control of my body and pushed myself to follow Dylan and Elizabeth, I heard Mr. Connors's aching call behind me.

"*Coral!*"

* * *

The door flew open as we raced up the stairs of the Mooring house. Lake glared out at us, steam practically coming out of his ears as he motioned for us to get inside. Once Dylan, Elizabeth, and I had tumbled into the house, Lake slammed the door, locking it and shoving the towels in front of the crack at the bottom again.

My body felt heavy and exhausted. I collapsed onto the couch and Mara rushed over, kneeling in front of me.

"Where have you been?" she exclaimed, her hands pawing over my arms and face, as if she were checking for injuries.

"Yes." Lake's voice was stern and tense. He crossed his arms as he looked down at me. "I'd like to know that myself."

Across the room, Dylan's parents were fussing over him. His mom examined him, then pulled him into a tight hug, her face pale. Mr. Waverly scowled, but the relief on his face made it less effective than Lake's glowering look.

A lump swelled in my throat and I broke my gaze from the reunion between Dylan and his parents.

"We went to talk to Elizabeth," I said.

All heads in the room—Lake, Mr. and Mrs. Waverly, Mara, Mr. Moody, and Sailor—turned toward the girl who had crumpled to the floor against the wall. She sat with her knees pulled up to her chest, apparently not caring that her pink-striped underwear was in full view. Her arms draped across her knees and her head was down, her hair shielding her face. It wasn't until her shoulders shook that I realized she was crying.

"Why?" Mara asked me.

I looked at her, then shifted my gaze to Dylan. She followed my gaze, and her expression changed. So she did know.

"We wanted to warn people," Dylan spoke up. "Elizabeth wouldn't answer my calls, and Mr. Connors had already hung up on Mr. Richter last night. I had to try to talk to Elizabeth in person, to get her to listen."

"Why is it any of your business whether the Connors girl is okay?" Mr. Moody growled, his eyes narrowed.

No one spoke for long moments. Dylan swallowed, his jaw tight.

Sailor looked between Dylan and Elizabeth, and then back again. She pushed herself up from the barstool where she had been sitting and laughed bitterly.

"Tell me you're joking," she said.

Dylan stared back at her, but he didn't speak.

"Elizabeth Connors?" Sailor roared. I cringed as her voice echoed off the walls around us. "You're in love with Elizabeth Connors?"

"I never said that," Dylan said quickly, his eyes darting toward Elizabeth, who was still huddled on the floor.

"Then what?" Sailor asked. "She's just your hook up buddy?"

Mr. Waverly's neck reddened and he cleared his throat. "Maybe we should discuss this later."

"We will discuss it later," Lake said, still glaring at Dylan and me. "You two are lucky Domnall didn't find you."

Dylan and I exchanged glances.

"Actually," I said, unable to meet Lake's gaze, "he did."

"We got away because of her." Dylan nodded toward Elizabeth.

"We were behind her house when the finfolk found us," I said. "Elizabeth came out to stop them, but she became caught up in the song. Then Mr. Connors came with his gun, but that was no use. Dylan and I were able to resist enough to

137

run and we brought Elizabeth with us. But they have her dad."

Lake pounded his fist on the wall. "Do you two understand what you're doing? Do you even *think* before you act?"

"They're children, Lake," Mrs. Waverly told him.

Dylan shrugged off his mom's hand. "We're not little kids. We do think, and we thought about what everyone else out there might be going through. We had to do something to try to warn them, to get someone to listen. We made it back in one piece, didn't we?"

Lake studied Dylan's face, his eyes narrowing. "That depends on your definition of one piece. What happened to your face?"

I had almost forgotten the fight we'd had. My eye throbbed at the reminder and I reached up to touch the area gingerly. Dylan's bottom lip was cut open in the middle and his cheek was red.

"Nothing," he said, looking quickly at me. "It's fine."

Lake ran a hand through his hair as he paced back and forth.

"We can't let them go rounding up all the humans on this island," Mr. Moody said, scratching at his beard. "If they build up an army of mindless people, we won't be any match for them at all."

"I know," Lake said.

"We can't hide out here forever," Mara added.

"I know!" Lake roared. He stopped pacing and sucked in a deep breath. "It doesn't seem that Callum is coming back. So we'll have to face them. On our own terms, not hiding out here like caged animals. We'll call everyone who will join us. Maybe we can fight back as a group."

I stood, nodding. "It's worth a shot."

Lake's glare sent an icy chill through me. "*You* are not going." He looked around at Mara, Dylan, and Sailor. "None of you. You're staying here."

"You can't leave us behind," Mara snapped.

"This is not a fight for children," her dad said. "You're not risking your life out there. You're staying here. That's final."

I was fine with Mara staying hidden, but I wasn't going to be left behind. "I'm not a child," I said. "I'm eighteen. And I'm not your son."

"You're my responsibility until your we get your mama back," Lake told me, his eyes flashing. He pointed at Sailor. "And I don't want to hear a word out of you either. Your grandma would agree with me if she were well enough."

"I agree with you," Mr. Moody spoke up, his eyes on Sailor. "She stays here."

"You let Callum go," I pointed out, not backing down from this argument with Lake. "He's only a year older than I am."

"Callum was not my responsibility," Lake said through clenched teeth. "You are, and I am not going to be the one to explain to your mama why I let you risk your life."

"It's my life to risk!" I shouted.

"I won't let you die like your father did!" Lake shouted back at me.

Silence fell over the room as we stared at each other. Lake's face was red, his eyes wide and wild, a haunted look in them. Then he shook his head. "You're staying here," he said in a softer tone. "That's my final word on it."

I started to open my mouth to argue more, but then closed it. Lake had his final say, but that didn't mean I had to listen.

Chapter 22

Lake, Mr. Moody, and Mr. and Mrs. Waverly all left to meet up with the rest of the finfolk and humans that would help them. They left Mr. Richter behind to keep an eye on the house. And us. No one said it out loud, but the clear implication was that Mr. Richter was our baby-sitter.

Once they had all left and Mr. Richter had gone back up to the attic lookout point, Dylan's little brother following along behind him, Sailor whirled around to face Dylan, her eyes dark and her hands on her hips.

"So," she said, looking him up and down. "Tell me."

"Tell you what?" Dylan asked.

Sailor glanced at Elizabeth, her nose wrinkling. "Tell me why you like her."

Dylan turned away from her. "Why do you care?"

"I've been your best friend since we were born, Dylan," Sailor said. "I've been right here, the whole time. But you never saw me the way you see Mara or *her*." She pointed at Elizabeth. "After everything she's said to me, the way she's treated me, how could you go behind my back and hook up with her?"

"You weren't here, Sailor," Dylan said. "Maybe I was bored."

Sailor laughed. "Mara was here. And Josh wasn't. So why not go after her?"

"Hey," Mara said, holding up her hands. "Leave us out of this."

I slipped my arm around Mara's waist, pulling her closer to me. I knew the jealousy that went through me at the thought of Mara and Dylan spending the summer here alone was irrational, but that didn't stop it from coming.

"So it was just something to do to pass your time?" Sailor asked, following Dylan as he walked toward the kitchen. "You were so worried about me you needed something to distract you, is that it?"

Elizabeth still sat on the floor, her head bent, but she had stopped crying.

"What do you want me to say?" Dylan asked. "Do you want me to say that I would have chosen you if you were here? I don't know. I don't think of you that way, Sailor. You're my best friend. You're like a sister to me."

Sailor stepped back, her mouth open. Those were the words she had never wanted to hear him say. She had told me before how much she loved him and had wanted him to notice her as more than just his friend. But he never had. I wasn't sure exactly how she felt about Callum, but I knew that Dylan's words had to hurt her.

"You have Callum anyway," Dylan muttered. "Why does it matter to you who I'm with when you brought him back here?"

Sailor's chin quivered. "Why her? Why do you want her?"

"He doesn't." Elizabeth wiped her cheeks, lifting her head and staring across the room at Dylan. "He doesn't want me. It was like you said, just something to help him pass the time. He made that very clear a few months ago."

"Is that true?" Sailor asked him. "You don't feel anything for her?"

Dylan ran a hand through his hair, shifting back and forth as the two girls stared at him. He looked like he was facing down an execution line.

I cleared my throat. "This little drama is fun to watch," I said, "but I think we have more important things to worry about."

Sailor held up one finger toward me. "No. Right now, we're talking about this."

"Yes," Elizabeth said. "I'd like to know how you really feel too, Dylan."

Mara gave me a worried look, then said, "We should probably—"

"No!" Sailor shouted. "Do you love her or not, Dylan?"

Dylan took a deep breath. "I—"

"What is all of this shouting?" a weak voice croaked.

All of us jumped at the sight of Miss Gale standing at the end of the hall, leaning against the wall. Coral stood on her other side, their arms linked. They blinked at us, looking around at each of our faces.

"Grandma," Sailor said, rushing over to her. "What are you doing out of bed?"

Miss Gale waved off Sailor's attempts to coddle her. "You expect me to stay in bed forever, child? I ain't stupid. I know there's things going on here that none of you want me to know about."

"How are you feeling?" Mara asked her.

Coral led Miss Gale over to the love seat and eased her down, then sat next to her mother, their hands still clasped.

"Better," Miss Gale said. "There are days and weeks I don't remember. But I'm feeling better." She smiled at Coral and then Sailor. "Now that I have my girls back, I'll be better."

Miss Gale looked around the room again. "Now," she said, letting out a long breath, "I think it's time someone started telling me what's happening here."

We looked at each other, waiting for someone to go first. What should we say? That we had led a group of finfolk who wanted to take over our home directly to the island? That it was August and probably no more than fifty degrees outside? That my mother had told me she killed my father?

There was so much to tell and maybe not enough time to explain it all.

Miss Gale's gaze settled on Sailor. "Tell me what happened after you left the island," she said.

Sailor sat down on the floor by her grandmother's knees, laying her head in Miss Gale's lap. She told Miss Gale about our swim across the ocean and our time in Westray. She told how we'd found Hether Blether with Callum's help, and about finding Coral there. I added my own observations to the story and tried to put all the pieces together in my head as I spoke, looking for anything that would help us save Swans Landing.

Then Mara and Dylan joined in as we told about what had happened in just the last few days. It seemed like it had been a lifetime since the finfolk had arrived on the island. It was hard to believe it had only been a day.

When we were done, Miss Gale cocked her head to the side. "Where is this key?" she asked.

I grabbed my bag and pulled it out, handing over the twisted piece of metal. Miss Gale turned it over in her hands, examining it with a furrowed brow.

"We need the key," Coral said, leaning her head against her mother's shoulder.

"What is it, sugar?" Miss Gale asked her gently. "Why do we need this key?"

"Oliver told me to get it," Coral said, her gaze shifting to me.

"What did I need it for, Coral?" I asked, kneeling down in front of her. "Can you remember?"

"It's the right key," she said. "I found it for you."

I stood, my shoulders slumping. She wasn't much better than she had been back in Hether Blether. Whatever had caused her confusion wasn't cured just by coming back home.

* * *

Each minute felt like an hour as we waited in the quiet house. The world outside was silent too, as if all life had disappeared from the island. Not even the caw of seagulls reached us.

"Do you think we'll know?" Mara asked me quietly. "If something happens to them, I mean. How will we know that they're not coming back?"

"They're coming back," Sailor snapped, glaring at Mara. "All of them."

I knew she meant Callum. She still held out hope that he was on our side and hadn't left us to join Domnall. I wasn't sure what to think anymore.

Miss Gale rubbed Sailor's back comfortingly. "They'll be back, sugar. We have to keep up hope." She looked so tired, but she refused to go back to bed, saying that she couldn't sleep while everything was so up in the air.

Mara ignored Sailor and leaned toward me, lowering her voice. "We need to do something. We can't sit and wait forever."

"We're not going to sit and wait," I said. "We're going to find an answer." I picked up my dad's papers. They were the only lead we had at the moment.

Mara settled into my corner with me, our backs pressed to the wall as we sat side by side. She took half of the stack of papers still left and I took the other one. Then I bent my head over the notes, trying to block out everyone else in the room.

Like before, most of the notes were about air and water temperatures, the weather for each day, and his observations about the sea life. If I had been searching for reasons why my father would have an affair, I couldn't find any. These papers were all pretty mundane, mostly facts and statistics. Why would he have Coral hide them?

September 5 - I'm learning to sing the finfolk song. I wasn't even sure that I had the ability to do it. I am part finfolk through my paternal grandmother, but I don't have the ability to change form like she did. My father couldn't change form either. I've thought a lot about the reasons why I feel so drawn to the ocean and the finfolk people, and I've theorized that even without the ability to change, some of the things that make one finfolk still exist inside me. The connection to the land and sea, for example.

I didn't want anyone else to know about my desire to learn the song if it turned out that I couldn't actually sing like they do, so I had to be discreet. During one of our morning rides out on the water to pull in catches, I asked Lake Westray if he would humor me and try to teach me the song.

I reread the last sentence again. My dad worked with Lake on the water? He had mentioned before that he often rode out with fisherman to observe their catches because it helped in his research of the fish population, but this was the first mention I'd seen that he had gone with Lake specifically.

Mara shifted next to me, her eyes scanning over the notebook in her hands. I wondered if I should tell her this fact. But I was eager to know more, so I turned back the page.

Lake was doubtful, of course, but he agreed. I've come to feel that I can trust him more than most people on the island. He's not someone who gets involved in local gossip.

I was able to pick up the melody of the song after only a couple of tries. The gold bursts in the corners of my eyes as I hummed told me I had found the right notes. I did it. As far as technicalities go, I am human. I don't change form in the ocean and I can't breathe the water. But I can sing, proving that even without the ability to change, a part of me is still finfolk inside.

145

I let the words I had just read seep into my head as a tingle spread through me. My dad could sing the songs. He wasn't just an ordinary human, even though he had appeared to be one. He had proven that a human with finfolk blood who couldn't change could still sing.

I scanned over the next few days' notes, skipping past more temperature readings and fish population notes. A word on one page—Finfolkaheem—caught my eye and I stopped.

November 21 - Observed a whirlpool near Pirate's Cove again today. It lasted only a brief moment before disappearing.

It's Song Night and the finfolk are out in the water. I'm sitting on the beach at Pirate's Cove, listening to them and studying the mists that always accompany this night.

I've been doing research on finfolk myths, though information is hard to find. Of course, there are no records written by finfolk about their origins—none that we have here in the human world, anyway. Maybe they keep those records in Finfolkaheem, but if so, no human eyes have ever seen them as far as I know.

I have developed theories about the vanishing isles that the finfolk are said to live on. My visit to Eynhallow didn't give me much observable evidence, so I can only go on guesses. Eynhallow—also known as Hildaland—is the only known island that is said to have once belonged to finfolk and was one of their vanishing isles until it was taken from them by humans. There is said to be at least one other island the finfolk still own, Hether Blether, though it remains hidden in the mists that protect it.

How can an island that once vanished become permanently visible to human eyes? We know that finfolk have taken humans—sometimes by force and sometimes willingly—to their islands throughout history, but just the presence of humans on the land doesn't make the island visible.

My theory is that Hildaland (Eynhallow) was not "taken" by humans, but was given up by the finfolk who once lived there. The mists come when the finfolk sing. Our population of finfolk here in Swans Landing is small, but what if there were a larger population on the island? Would the mists that appear on Song Night stick around longer? Permanently?

The finfolk who inhabited Hildaland gave up the island for whatever reason, and without their song the mists faded and the island became visible to humans. I can only guess that they either went home to Finfolkaheem as a permanent residence, or they combined with the finfolk of Hether Blether.

My heart pounded in my ears as I skimmed over the next pages, looking for more of my dad's theories about the finfolk. He was right. Domnall had told me himself that the song protected Hether Blether. With fewer finfolk, the song's power faded and that was why Domnall claimed he needed the Swans Landing finfolk.

But I didn't think that the Hildaland finfolk had gone to Hether Blether. If they had, there would have been more of them still there. Hether Blether was dying out with such a small community after the split that had caused our ancestors to come to Swans Landing. That had to mean that the Hildaland finfolk had gone to Finfolkaheem.

But where was it? How could I find the door?

November 27 - I've been rereading the finfolk myths again. One stuck out at me this time. The myth of the finfolk key. It is said that a human girl was taken by finfolk to Hether Blether. Her father and brother had gone out to look for her, but were unable to find her. During a storm, their little boat became lost in the mists and they found their way to the vanishing isle, where the girl greeted them. Before they left, she gave them a twisted piece of metal that she said would bring them back to Hether Blether in the future.

What if this key led not only to the vanishing isle, but to the finfolk home under the ocean?

November 30 – The whirlpool reappeared and Coral swam out to it. She said it sucked her under, the current so rough that she almost couldn't control herself. Near the bottom was a light and as she neared it, it grew larger, opening like a door. Her own fear made her fight to get away and come back to shore. I won't ask her to go into the light, whatever it is, but my thoughts about the finfolk key have my mind spinning with possibilities.

December 7 — We've been trying to find the whirlpool again, but it hasn't reappeared. It seems to be random, but maybe it isn't. If it was a door, like Coral thought, shouldn't there be a way to open it on command?

Shouldn't there be a key?

Mara looked up at me as I leapt to my feet. "What's wrong?"

"I know how to get to Finfolkaheem," I said.

Dylan had been lying on the couch, staring up at the ceiling, but now he raised his head to look at me. "What are you talking about?"

"The finfolk homeland," I said. "Not the vanishing isles, but the city under the sea. Where the finfolk originated long ago, long before the vanishing isles came into existence. I know how to get there. At least, I think I do."

I grabbed my bag and fished the key out, squeezing my hand around the twisted metal. Coral was right all along. We needed the key.

Mara stood and grabbed my arm, spinning me around to face her. "Wait," she said. "Why would we go to Finfolkaheem? Is there something there that can help us?"

"I don't know," I told her. "But it's the only option we have right now."

Sailor studied me from her position on the love seat. "We're not supposed to leave the house, remember? We're being baby-sat."

"I don't care," I said. "For all we know, everyone else is either dead or under Domnall's control. I'm going to find the way to Finfolkaheem, and if I find the rest of the finfolk there, I'm asking for their help."

Miss Gale watched me from her seat, her mouth set into a straight line and her forehead creased in thought.

"I'm sorry," I told her. "I don't meant to disobey you, but we can't sit here forever when we may be able to find help."

Miss Gale shook her head. "You're not disobeying me, sugar. Go, find help. Lord knows we need it."

I looked at her for a long moment, frozen in shock. Miss Gale wasn't going to stop me. She had given me permission to break Lake's rules and leave the house.

I rushed forward, leaning down to wrap my arms around Miss Gale, hugging her frail body tight. "Thank you," I whispered.

Miss Gale let out a long, weary breath. "No sense in me stopping you anyway, is there, sugar?" She pulled back and smiled up at me. "Your daddy would be proud of the man you've become," she whispered.

My vision blurred and I blinked quickly to keep the tears back.

Elizabeth pushed herself up from the space on the floor where she had sat the whole time. "I'm going with you."

"You can't," I said. "You're not finfolk."

"I'm not staying here," she said through clenched teeth. "They have my daddy. I'm going with you as far as I can."

I sighed. "Fine."

"I'm going too," Mara spoke up. She shot me a look like she dared me to protest.

"So am I," Sailor said as she stood.

Dylan let out a frustrated sigh. "Well, I'm certainly not getting left behind again." He sat up and raised his eyebrows. "How do we get out of here without Mr. Richter knowing?"

I pressed my lips together as I thought about this obstacle. Then I said, "Is your little brother still upstairs?"

Dylan nodded. "Should be. Why?"

"How good is he at providing distractions?"

Chapter 23

"I want to go too." Reed crossed his arms and glared up at his brother.

Dylan sighed. "I already told you, you have to stay here and provide the distraction."

Reed shook his head. "No way. I'm going with you. It's boring sitting here all day."

We weren't even out of the house yet and already the plan was in danger.

"I'll give you twenty bucks to stay here," I said.

He tilted his head to the side and tapped a finger on his chin. "Fifty," he said.

What did this kid think I was, an ATM? I reached into my pocket and pulled out a couple of crumpled bills. "I have twenty bucks. Take it or leave it."

Reed scowled, but he snatched the money from my hand and stuffed it into his pocket. "You got a deal." He smirked at his brother. "At least someone around here knows how to negotiate."

He slid off the barstool and then disappeared into the hall. I heard the door to the attic close and then the muffled sound of his footsteps going up the stairs.

"Okay," I said, "now we just have to get out of here without being seen."

"We did it once before," Dylan said. "Should be easy."

The only problem was that when Dylan and I had snuck out the first time, it had been 6:00 A.M. and most people were still asleep. Now it was after eleven A.M. I worried about who might be looking out their windows, or where the finfolk and everyone else might be. We had to get to Pirate's Cove without running into anyone that might try to stop us.

The five of us slipped out of the back door of the Mooring house, moving as softly as we could to keep our footsteps from being too loud. The afternoon was cold and windy, and my eyes watered at the blast of icy air that hit me once I was outside.

We didn't speak as we raced across the backyard toward the house directly behind the Mooring home. I barely even dared to breathe. At any moment, I expected Domnall to step out of a shadow or from behind a tree. I was the oldest of the group assembled behind me and I was leading them all into danger. If anything happened to them, I didn't think I'd ever forgive myself.

We made it out of the neighborhood without any problems. The streets were empty. There was no sign of the finfolk or of Lake and the others. Was that a good thing or bad?

As we dashed past businesses and trees along Heron Avenue, a figure appeared in the path ahead of us. A small, blonde figure stood there, facing us as we skidded to a stop.

"Claire," Mara said. She started forward. "Claire, what are you doing out here? There are people—"

I grabbed her arm, stopping her in her tracks. Another figure stood nearby, half-hidden next to an old, abandoned store. He stepped out of the shadows, the wind whipping the hem of his robe around his legs.

Artair, Domnall's guard.

"Let her go," I called to him. "She's just a kid."

Artair gazed back at me. He was too far away to hear, but I was sure he was humming and keeping Claire under the trance of the song. We had never used the song to control humans, but I wondered what it was capable of making them do. What could a finfolk who had much more experience with the song use it for? My stomach twisted at the empty, glazed look in Claire's eyes.

I scanned the area around us, but we were alone. It was just us and Artair and Claire, standing on the empty main street of Swans Landing. I dug my fingers into Mara's arm, shifting my position so that my body partially blocked her.

Then Artair moved, but he didn't come toward us. Instead, he turned away and walked back into the shadows of the shop. Claire stood there for a moment, then she too turned and followed Artair, disappearing from sight.

"What's he doing?" Sailor asked.

I shook my head. "I don't know."

My body was rigid as I waited for the attack I was certain would come. My gaze darted from right to left and back again, searching the shadows for movement. My ears strained to hear any sound other than the wind whistling past us.

But there was nothing.

"I…I think he's letting us go," I said at last.

Mara raised her eyebrows. "Why would he do that?"

"We don't have time to question it," Dylan said. "We need to get out of here. Now."

Our feet pounded against the asphalt as we raced toward Pirate's Cove. We reached the little parking lot at the edge of the trees and I was relieved to see it was empty. I had half-expected to find everyone there fighting, or an ambush waiting for us.

Tree limbs scratched at my face and arms as I ran down the narrow dirt path that wound through the maritime forest. Elizabeth tripped over a tree limb and Dylan paused to grab her hand, pulling her to her feet before continuing.

My lungs felt like they were in danger of bursting by the time we broke free of the forest and reached the little sliver of beach. The ocean roared and foamed as it crashed onto the shore, the water almost as gray as the sky overhead.

"What do we do now?" Mara asked me. "How do we get to Finfolkaheem?"

The five of us stood at the edge of the water. I could already feel the ocean soaking through my shoes and my body responding to the call of it.

"We need to swim," I said, kicking off my shoes and then pulling off my socks. "There's a whirlpool. My dad wrote about it, and Dylan and I found it the other day. I think it's part of the door."

"A door?" Dylan asked as he pulled his shirt off over his head. "In the ocean?"

"Callum told Sailor and me that Hether Blether once had a door to Finfolkaheem," I explained, speaking quickly as we all stripped down. "My dad wrote about the finfolk homeland and his theories about the song. It doesn't just call finfolk home, it creates the mists that protect the vanishing isles. That's what we've been doing all these years, every time we sing we're turning Swans Landing into a vanishing island. That's why the fish are disappearing and why the ferry isn't coming. The island is vanishing from the human world."

Mara froze, her hands on the waist of her jeans. "That's insane. How can the island vanish?"

"It's happened before," I said. "Domnall told me that the finfolk sing to protect Hether Blether and with the declining population there, their protection is fading. What if ours here is growing? And if it is and we are turning Swans Landing into a vanishing island, then it must have a connection to the city under the sea now. We have the key. We can open the door."

I pulled the key from the pocket of my jeans before tossing them into the sand and squeezed it tight. It *had* to work. If it didn't, I was out of ideas. I didn't know what else my dad might have wanted me to find if it wasn't this.

"What about me?" asked a voice behind us.

Elizabeth stood on the beach, her hands crossed as she scowled at us. "I can't breathe underwater, remember? What am I supposed to do, wait here?"

Dylan, Mara, Sailor, and I looked at each other.

"You'll have to," I told her. "Sorry. If we find Finfolkaheem, you wouldn't survive being under water that long."

Elizabeth's chin quivered. "And what if these finfolk freaks find me waiting here? What do I do then?"

I bit my lip. Elizabeth would have no chance of resisting if Domnall found her. Maybe Artair wasn't really letting us go. Maybe he had gone to find the others and bring them back to us.

Dylan walked across the sand toward Elizabeth. He reached around the back of her head and then pulled her face toward his, kissing her for a long moment. Sailor turned away, closing her eyes as she faced the ocean.

When Dylan pulled away, he said, "If they come, you run. Hide anywhere you can, any place that you can block out the sound of the song. We'll be back as soon as we can."

Elizabeth nodded and kissed him one last time before stepping back.

"Hold hands," I said, reaching for Mara's hand. She grasped Dylan's and then he reached for Sailor.

Sailor looked at him for a moment, her jaw clenched tight. Then she slipped her hand into his.

"Whatever you do, stick together," I said. "I have the key. It should lead us to where we need to go."

Then the four of us stepped into the crashing waves.

* * *

154

Water gurgled in my ears once my head had slipped under the water. The current pushed me one way and then the other. I had to squeeze Mara's hand tight to keep from losing her.

Then the change overtook me. I opened my mouth, letting out a stream of bubbles as my body shifted and popped, tore and stretched. I twisted, bucking at the pain. Mara's fingers started to slip through my grasp. My brain was foggy, unable to focus as the change seized me, but I tried to hold on as best I could.

Finally, the change was over and I was finfolk. Pain ebbed away, clearing my mind enough that I could remember what I was looking for.

Finfolkaheem. We had to find the door, if it was here. If my dad's theories and my guesses were right, and Swans Landing was turning into a vanishing isle, Finfolkaheem might be our only solution. We needed full-blooded finfolk, as Callum had said, and this was the only place I knew to find them.

The four of us swam forward, pushing against the current that tried to tug us back toward the beach. I gripped the key in my fist, focusing all my thoughts on it as we swam, like I had seen Callum do when we were searching for Hether Blether.

I knew we had found the whirlpool when the current suddenly changed and pushed me toward the right, sending me almost tumbling through the water. I wanted to tell the others to hold on tighter, but speaking underwater was impossible. Only bubbles came out when I opened my mouth, and I didn't know if they could have heard me anyway over the roaring water around us. The sea was ferocious and battered us back and forth.

Where is it? I asked silently. *Where's the door?*

The water pushed at me again, snatching my hand from Mara's. I fought to get back to her, my arm swinging wildly through the current. I couldn't lose them now.

But the current was too strong and the water too dark. I couldn't see anyone near me or find her hand.

"Mara!" I called, but my shout disappeared in the explosion of bubbles from my mouth. I swung my arm out again, searching for anyone, slicing at the water around me.

Finally, my hand found something solid. An arm. I grabbed hold, squeezing my fingers around the limb. I wouldn't lose them again. The water swirled around me, sending me spinning in violent circles.

We needed the door. Where was the door?

A brightness seared through the water under my feet. I peered down at it as I spun on the current. The light was first just an outline, then an entire circle that shone brilliantly. Where there had been only complete darkness moments ago, there was now a golden light like I had never seen before.

Still holding onto the person's arm with one hand and the finfolk key in the other, I dove down, swimming and fighting to get through the water to reach the door.

Chapter 24

The gold light was so brilliant I couldn't keep my eyes open. I squeezed them shut, hanging onto whoever's arm I had hold of. I drifted through the current that pulled me into the light, wondering for a moment if all the stories about death were true. Maybe this wasn't the way to Finfolkaheem after all. Maybe instead of going toward the light we should have fought to swim away.

But then the light faded, leaving me with residual spots in the darkness behind my eyelids.

Slowly, my body still tensed, I opened my eyes to look around.

It was immediately clear that we were no longer in the water just off Swans Landing. The water here was the clearest I had ever seen. The Atlantic Ocean around Swans Landing was murky and it was hard to see more than a couple of feet. But the ocean floor spread out for miles around me, the hills and rocks and fish and plant life all easily visible. Before us, in the valley between craggy cliffs, lay a city built from rock and sand, lit with a strange blue glow.

Mara, Dylan, and Sailor floated next to me. It was Dylan's arm I was holding and I let go, reaching for Mara's hand instead. She raised her eyebrows, her face showing the same question that went through my head. Was this Finfolkaheem?

It had to be. There was no place else it could be.

But what should we do now that we were here? The key I still clenched in one fist had gotten us here, but I couldn't feel any more direction coming from it.

Two figures appeared floating down from above us. They were finfolk, the man with glittering silver scales and the woman with a mix of blue and green. They both had long hair that floated loose in the water around their heads like a halo.

Memories of our arrival in Hether Blether flashed through my head. We had been taken to the palace by armed sentries who had found us, and then we had been imprisoned for a few days by Domnall. My body went rigid as the two finfolk swam toward us, their faces stern as they studied us.

"You will come with us," said the woman, speaking in a musical tone. She nodded to her companion and then they turned, swimming toward the city.

The rest of us exchanged glances. Sailor looked as nervous as I felt, probably remembering what had happened in Hether Blether too. But these finfolk were not armed, and when they realized we weren't following, they stopped and gestured to us.

"It is all right," the man said. "We are taking you to speak to the council. That is why you are here, correct?"

I didn't know what the council was, but it seemed like the best place to start to ask for help. I opened my mouth to say yes, but found that I still couldn't speak underwater. The two finfolk made it look easy, like it should have been natural. But the only thing that came out of my mouth was a muffled noise and bubbles. So I nodded instead and then the four of us followed them toward the city.

Hether Blether had reminded me of Swans Landing when I first saw it. Not the sandstone palace, but the decaying village that sat around it. The people there had been fighting to hang onto their homes and history, just like the people of Swans Landing had been doing for years. The two places had had a lot of similarities between them, though it had taken me too long to realize just how similar they were.

But Finfolkaheem was entirely different. The city stretched on and on, dipping into valleys in the ocean floor and climbing up the sides of the cliffs. Seaweed drifted around us and lush plants grew up from the sandy floor, climbing over the rock walls of homes and buildings as if it were decoration put there on purpose. It took me a moment to realize that the city's glow wasn't from any kind of lights that I had ever seen above the water, but from the algae that grew on the rocks and ocean floor. The bacteria gave off a phosphorescent blue light that lit the paths between the homes.

A song hung in the air around us, songs of water and earth combined into something I had never heard before. Tension left my body as the song vibrated through me, renewing me with a calmness that settled deep inside me.

A little school of bright yellow fish darted out of the way as we drew close to the center of the city. Finfolk milled about the area, some sitting on rock ledges to talk and children chasing each other in circles.

All movement stopped once they spotted us following the other two finfolk into the village square. All I could do was stare back at hundreds of eyes that stared at us. I had never seen so many finfolk in one place. The color of finfolk scales were based on family lines and most family members had similar colors. There were only a few different colors still left in Swans Landing, but here there were more variations of colors than I had ever thought possible.

The man and woman who had found us approached a stone circle where four men and women floated together. They were older than most of the finfolk there, with long white streams of hair floating around their heads. They wore necklaces made of seashells, large conch shells in front.

"We found visitors who came through the door," the woman said.

The men and women turned to us, their eyes looking us up and down. I knew how dangerous finfolk could be, but I didn't feel afraid. The song in the water had eased all of my worries. Everything was all right. We were safe here.

"Welcome to Finfolkaheem," one of the men said, smiling at us. "We are the council, the judges here in the city. I am Finlay. These are my companions, Iomhar, Mairead, and Sorcha."

Finlay looked at us expectantly, as if waiting for our introductions. I opened my mouth, letting out a stream of bubbles and shaking my head as I pointed to my throat.

The woman called Mairead nodded. "Ah, you cannot speak underwater. You are not the first to come here with that problem. You have human blood, aye? It is one of the weaknesses the human part of you introduces into the finfolk form. We can repair you."

The four men and women closed their eyes, and a hum drifted toward us. My body tingled and my throat warmed. I touched my neck, expecting it to be hot, but the skin felt cool in the tepid water around me.

When the humming stopped, the council looked at us, expectant smiles on their faces.

Mara, Dylan, and Sailor looked back at me with blank faces. What had the finfolk done to us?

Mara coughed. "Can we talk now?" she asked. Her voice sounded different, more musical and lower, but she spoke clearly, just as the finfolk did. Her eyes widened.

"You changed us," I said to the council.

Mairead inclined her head. "I am sorry if it was unwanted. We have met others with your condition and assumed that you would want the change."

"What did you do?" Sailor asked, rubbing her throat.

"The song can be used to change the way your body works in connection with your mind," Finlay said. "You had the ability to speak underwater all along, but your human heritage did not allow you to remember how to do it. We merely told the finfolk genes inside you how to override the humanness in your vocal chords."

"Like how Domnall kept Callum from changing form," I said to Sailor.

Iomhar nodded. "That is one of the ways the song can be used, though it is not used often. It is considered the ultimate punishment for a finfolk to be unable to change form." His eyes narrowed as he looked at us. "Who among your people has been doing this?"

"Not our people," Dylan said quickly. "Domnall is from Hether Blether."

A murmur spread through the crowd in the square at his words.

Sorcha's eyebrows rose. "We lost contact with the vanishing isle long ago," she said. "The door closed there, but one opens at another location from time to time."

"In Swans Landing," I said. "That's where we came from. You said we're not the first finfolk you've met with human blood. Are there others from our island here?"

Mairead gestured toward the city around us. "There are others of your kind here. Ones who found their way home, though it has been a while since anyone has come here from your island. But you are welcome. All finfolk are welcome in our city."

We wouldn't be thrown into a prison like we had been in Hether Blether upon our arrival there. I could see relief and contentment in the faces of my friends as well. Sailor smiled as she floated in the water next to me. The song whispered through my body, erasing my fears. Why had I been afraid? Everything here was good. We could be happy here, no one could ever hurt us.

Finlay smiled, as if he understood everything going through my head. "Welcome home, young ones."

Chapter 25

I let myself float along with the gentle current that flowed through Finfolkaheem. I felt so relaxed, in a way I never had before. Why had I been so tense? Whatever it was, it didn't matter now. I was safe. Mara and Sailor were safe.

Mara floated at my side, her eyes closed and a soft smile on her face. Her black curls drifted in the water around her head. She looked so beautiful, so peaceful. I moved toward her, slipping my arms around her waist. She opened her eyes and her smile stretched wider when she saw it was me.

"Hey, you," she said, laughing a little.

"Hey." I pressed my lips on hers and she kissed me back, wrapping her arms around my neck. The finfolk council had given us a room—a suite, really. A collection of rooms all to ourselves, decorated in brightly colored sea anemones and fluorescent algae that grew in swirling patterns on the rock walls. We had everything we could need in these rooms, including food. All given to us freely. The finfolk here were so nice, so much nicer than…

Than who? Who was it I was trying to think of?

"What's wrong?" Mara asked when I pulled away from her.

I furrowed my brow as I tried to focus on the thought that was already slipping away into the recesses of my mind. I couldn't remember who wasn't as nice as the finfolk here.

"Nothing," I said, shaking my head. It didn't matter anyway, whatever it was. It couldn't have been important.

I kissed Mara again, flicking my tail to pull her toward the collection of sea sponges that served as a kind of bed. We floated just above the sponges, my hands roaming over the curve of her hip and the slickness of her golden brown scales. I didn't know where Sailor and Dylan had gotten off to, and at the moment, I didn't care.

"I love you, Josh," she whispered in my ear, letting out a stream of bubbles that tickled my skin.

Her words and the constant humming song that hung in the air around us filled me with a swell of happiness. "I love you too," I told her, knowing it was true. I had loved her from the moment I met her, swimming at Pirate's Cove.

No, wait. Not *swimming*. We'd had…What were they called? Legs? We'd been standing on the beach when we first met, hadn't we? It seemed impossible to think of myself ever having legs. I looked down at my silver tail, flicking it back and forth.

"Josh?" Mara's forehead was creased into a frown as she studied me. "Are you okay?"

"Did we…" The question seemed ridiculous, but I had to ask it. "Did we walk on land? With…legs?"

My head felt so fuzzy. I couldn't focus on anything. Already, the thought was slipping away again, and I laughed at myself, at the ridiculousness of my question.

But Mara wasn't laughing. She bit her lip, her eyes narrowed. "Walking?" she asked. "I think…I remember something. Sand. And…trees?"

But even as she spoke the words, her expression relaxed and her eyes took on the distant, contented look they had before. She reached for me again, pressing her lips to mine.

Part of me was still a little tense, but I kissed her back, letting myself relax into her embrace.

This was good. This was the way it was supposed to be, the two of us together, happy and safe.

Safe from what?

I kissed Mara harder, driving the thoughts out of my head. It didn't matter. I was with Mara and I loved her and we would be together here in Finfolkaheem forever. We would get married one day. Have a few kids. I could be a father.

A father.

My father.

My father...

No. The image that flashed into my head wasn't my father. It was my mother.

I jerked backward, crashing into the rock wall. Mara stared wide-eyed at me, her lips swollen and red.

"Josh?" she asked, reaching toward me. "What's wrong?"

The song filled my head and I felt myself relaxing. No. I didn't want to relax. I had to hang onto the thought. My mother...my mother in trouble.

My mother trapped by...Domnall.

"The song," I said, pressing the heels of my palms into my forehead. "We have to fight against the song. It's making us forget."

"Forget what?" Mara asked. She laughed as she swam toward me. "Josh, you're acting weird. Come back to bed with me. Everything is all right."

I shook my head. "No, it's not! We're forgetting why we came here." I grabbed her arms, squeezing my fingers into her skin as I fought against the haziness that licked at my mind. "Mara, think! Remember Swans Landing. Remember the finfolk there. Remember your dad and Miss Gale."

I didn't know how, but the city and the song were making it hard for us to remember anything above the surface. I struggled to hold onto the thoughts of Swans Landing. We had to find help and get back to the island.

Mara looked confused, but she said, "Lake?"

I nodded. "Right. Remember why we're here. We need to get help." Everything was coming back to me, fighting through the haze the song had settled over my mind.

Mara's eyes became clear with understanding. "We need to get out of here."

"Let's find Sailor and Dylan," I said, hoping we could fight off the song's effects long enough to find the help we needed.

* * *

Silence fell over the square after we had finished explaining everything that was happening in Swans Landing. Mara and I had found Sailor and Dylan, swimming aimlessly through the alleys of Finfolkaheem. It had taken a lot of talking to get them to remember who they were and why we were here, but the four of us continued to fight against the effects of the song. All around us, I could now see how the people of Finfolkaheem moved with glazed, contented expressions on their faces. It was no wonder that no one who had left Swans Landing in the past had ever returned. If they had found their way here to Finfolkaheem, the song probably had them under its spell. It would be so easy to be like them, to let the song soothe away all of my worries and just forget about life above the surface. But we couldn't do that, we couldn't leave Swans Landing to Domnall.

I had told about what I'd learned from my dad's papers, and Sailor and I had told about our journey to Hether Blether, while Mara and Dylan talked about the changes in Swans Landing's weather and how the ferry had stopped coming. Then we spoke about Domnall and the Hether Blether finfolk.

It was a long story, and it was hard to keep track of time. The song still made my thoughts fuzzy and every now and then one of us would trail off, blinking in confusion, until someone else reminded them of where we were. Each minute that we remained underwater was another minute things could go terribly wrong above the surface. Another minute for Elizabeth to be found and taken like the other humans. Another minute for us to lose any chance we might have. We had already lost too much time.

The crowd assembled around us seemed to be holding their breath, all eyes on the four men and women of the council. But even they didn't speak.

I flicked my tail back and forth. "We need your help," I said again. "We don't know how to defeat Domnall when he can use the song against us. Please. Come back to Swans Landing with us. You can do something."

The four exchanged long looks. Then Finlay spoke. "We will not leave Finfolkaheem."

"Why not?" Mara asked, her voice tinged with defeat.

"Our people do not walk on land any longer," Mairead said. "We saw how the human world corrupted our people and killed our lands. When we left Hildaland for the last time, we left for good to save ourselves. Finfolkaheem is connected to both land and water, and we can satisfy our urges for them here on the ocean floor. We no longer visit your world. We will not leave Finfolkaheem."

An icy chill spread down my spine. Without their help, we didn't have much of a chance of defeating Domnall.

"You have to come with us," I said. "We can't let Domnall take our home. He's controlling humans. Our friends and family."

"We are sorry," Sorcha said. "But we cannot go. If there are others here who would be willing to return to the surface with you, you may ask them."

I felt the eyes of hundreds of finfolk watching us from all around the cliff walls. Even the children had stopped playing and studied us with blank faces.

"Please!" Sailor shouted, her face crinkled into a deep frown. "We need your help!"

But no one came forward. No one spoke.

"Your people are welcome to seek refuge here with us," Finlay said. "We welcome all of our kind, even those who are lost."

"What about the humans?" Dylan asked. "We're supposed to leave them behind with these other finfolk controlling them?"

Mairead shrugged. "The humans have never shown concern for our kind, so we have no concern for them either. We know you carry human blood, and it is through no fault of your own that your people mingled with the humans. But we do not involve ourselves in the affairs of the surface walkers."

"It's our home," I said. "How do you expect us to leave it?"

"We left our home," Sorcha said. "We gave Hildaland to the humans. You will learn to call Finfolkaheem home, just as our people have."

"We're not leaving our friends behind," Dylan said through clenched teeth.

I shook my head at the council. "I'm sorry, but we can't give up our island so easily."

"I remember that island," a voice in the crowd said.

A woman swam forward, her silver scales sparkling in the light of the algae as she passed. Her face was lined with wrinkles that even the water couldn't smooth away, and even though everyone else kept their hair unbound, she had hers in a dark braid that trailed behind her in the water.

Her face was familiar, though I couldn't figure out why.

"The humans control that island," she said. "They berate us and treat us like we're not even people. You know that. All of you should know that."

"You're Nora Moray," Dylan said, his eyes widening as he looked at the woman.

My head whipped back to her and I studied her face closer. I had only a vague memory of the woman swimming before us. She had left Swans Landing when I was young. She

167

was a cousin of mine through my father's grandmother. No one had ever heard from her again. We hadn't found her in Hether Blether either. We hadn't found anyone that had left our island there except for Sailor's mom.

"Yes, I am," she answered. "I left your island because I was tired of being treated like I was nothing. Think about everything the humans have put you through. You can save the rest of the finfolk by bringing them here, where they'll be happy and can live with their own kind. Leave the humans to whatever fate awaits them. Finfolkaheem is where you belong, where you can be happy."

She made it sound so simple. The humans had mistreated the finfolk for a long time. Maybe it was just the way humans were. It was what they had always done to each other all throughout history, so why should we expect them to treat us any differently?

The Hether Blether finfolk called the mixed human blood a weakness. Finfolk belonged with each other. We could protect each other and be happy. We could be safe.

But I had to go back to Swans Landing….Didn't I?

"We can't do that," I told her, shaking away the haziness that had filled my head. "Yes, the humans have been unfair to the finfolk. But this isn't simply a matter of finfolk versus human. We—" I gestured between myself and Mara and Dylan and Sailor. "—are not just finfolk. We're human too. And some of the humans up there are our friends and family. We have to help them."

Nora shook her head. "Then you will do it on your own. Those of us who left have no intentions of ever going back."

She swam past us, disappearing into the alley between two rows of homes.

The last bit of hope I'd had disappeared as Nora swam out of sight.

"I guess that's it then," Mara said, reaching for my hand.

I nodded. "We have to go back. Maybe it's not too late."

The fourth council member, Iomhar, who had been silent while the others spoke to us, cleared his throat.

"There may be a way that you can save your people," Iomhar said.

I didn't dare hope. I didn't want to be disappointed again. "How?" I asked.

"These finfolk from Hether Blether, they are resistant to the song because they have no human blood," Iomhar said. "Your people are of mixed heritage and therefore, are vulnerable to the song's effects in the way that humans are."

I nodded. "Right. So how do we defeat them when they can use the song against us?"

"You cannot," Iomhar said.

Mara started to swim toward the older finfolk, her face contorted into a scowl, but I held her back. "If you can't help us, don't pretend you can," she snapped.

Iomhar shook his head. "I mean, you cannot defeat them as you are now. But you could, if you were fully finfolk."

I frowned. "How can we do that?"

"You need to be immune to the song's effects," Iomhar said. "You need pure finfolk blood. You need to be *remade*."

Sorcha looked sharply at Iomhar. "No one has attempted that in a long time. We have never sung that song."

"It will take a lot of effort," Finlay added.

Iomhar gestured around the square. "We have plenty of energy to help us do it."

"Do what exactly?" Sailor asked. "Is it like when my friend Callum couldn't change to finfolk form? Domnall used a song to keep him human."

Iomhar tilted his head. "That is only a surface change, and takes less energy than what I am proposing. What your friend went through is only a block in the mind that would keep the body in one form. This, however, would be a complete rebirth of your entire body and mind. The song recreates the structure of your body from the inside, erasing the human parts and turning them finfolk."

"So Domnall wouldn't be able to use the song against us," I said. "It wouldn't manipulate our minds the way it does now."

Iomhar nodded. "Precisely. You would be on level ground against him."

It was the only option we had. All of the finfolk in Swans Landing had some human blood in them, so we were all susceptible to Domnall's song. Callum might have been the only full finfolk on our side, but he was just one person and we didn't know what had happened to him. We needed as many as we could get.

Just as I opened my mouth to agree to the change, Iomhar held up his hand.

"There is one warning I must give you before you agree," he said. "If you undergo the change, it will be permanent. Everything that makes you as you are now will be irreversibly changed. There will be no way to turn the finfolk genes back to the blended human form you have now. You will be reborn as a new, fully finfolk person and will erase all evidence of your human ancestry."

Chapter 26

Finfolkaheem was a beautiful city. As the four of us swam through the alleys between the homes, I took in all the engravings etched along the sides of the rock to try to keep my thoughts grounded on something. If I let my mind wander, I could feel the effects of the song in the water threatening to take over. I couldn't afford to lose anymore time here.

Finfolk history was carved into stone, pictures showing finfolk throughout the years. Some were crude and worn until parts of them had disappeared. Others were newer, the lines deep but already being smoothed by the water that constantly passed over it. Even here, finfolk history could be erased over time, changed to suit the beliefs of newer generations.

"So what do you think?" Mara asked.

Sailor paused, reaching out to brush her hand over a cluster of bright pink and orange anemones that grew along the side of a home. The spindly tips swayed back and forth, as if waving at her. "I'll do to save Swans Landing," she said.

We had asked for time to think over the offer. Time wasn't something we really had much of, but this kind of decision wasn't something we could rush into. If we agreed to be changed, we would face a lifetime in our new bodies. We'd leave behind part of our families' heritage.

How would it feel? Would we know that a part of us was gone?

I put my hand on her shoulder, squeezing a little. "You don't have to. I'll do it."

Mara narrowed her eyes at me. "You don't sound worried."

I shrugged and turned away from her.

Mara swam over to me, until our faces were only inches apart. "Why are you doing it?" she asked.

"Like Sailor said. To save Swans Landing."

She shook her head. "Besides that."

"Does it matter?" I asked.

Her gaze flicked toward Sailor and she asked, "Did you tell your sister what happened to your father?"

Sailor raised her eyebrows. "What? Josh? What is she talking about?"

When I didn't say anything, Mara said, "He knows who killed Oliver Canavan."

"Who?" Sailor grabbed my arm, digging her nails into my skin. "Tell me. You *have* to tell me. This is my father too."

I closed my eyes, swallowing. Then I said, "My mom."

When I opened my eyes, three saddened faces looked back at me. Sailor let go of me, blinking as she shrank back.

"When were you going to tell me?" she asked.

I shrugged. "When all of this was over. There's too much else to worry about right now."

Sailor's forehead was scrunched into a deep scowl. "What happened?"

I sighed. "Do we have to talk about this now?"

"Yes," Sailor said. "Since you don't seem to want to talk about it any other time."

I shot Mara an annoyed scowl, then turned back to Sailor. "She was already unstable back then, I think. My mom found our dad on the pier that night, waiting for your mom. She pushed him off. He hit his head on the pilings and drowned. That's it. I don't know that she really meant to kill him. She probably wasn't even thinking rationally." I ripped up a handful of seaweed and tossed it into the current. "It doesn't matter anyway." I shot a glare at Mara. "Why did you even bring this up?"

"Because you're afraid of the human part of you," Mara said, crossing her arms.

"No, I'm not."

"You think the human part of your dad was what made him weak and made him have an affair," Mara said. "And now you know your human mother killed your father. So you'll give up the human part of you because you think it will keep you from doing the wrong things."

"I'm trying to save Swans Landing," I said.

"So why didn't you tell Sailor what you know?" Mara asked. "Why haven't you let her see your dad's papers? Why do you keep looking for an answer that isn't there?"

I clenched my teeth, running my fingers over the lines carved in the wall next to me.

Mara wrapped her arms around me, resting her chin on my shoulder. "You are not your parents, Josh. What they did doesn't change who you are. Being finfolk or being human won't change that either."

"It's a weakness," I told her, pushing out of her embrace. "Domnall said it was, even the council said it. Maybe they're right."

Mara followed as I swam ahead. "Domnall is a lot of things, but right isn't one of them. Don't give up part of yourself just because you're afraid it will make you into something you don't want to be. That's not who you are. It's not who you will be. We are more than the blood that runs in our veins."

I spun around, whipping up an eruption of bubbles around me. "I don't want to be afraid of being human, but I don't know what I am anymore. I lived one life pretending to

173

be human. Now I'm trying to figure out how to be who I really am."

Mara laughed. "You think I don't know exactly what you're going through? The girl who didn't know she was finfolk until six months ago?"

Of course she knew. It was what had drawn me to her when she first arrived on the island. She wasn't like anyone else. If anyone knew how I felt, it was her.

"So," Mara said, taking a deep breath. "We need to decide. Not because of anyone else or because of fear or anger, but because the people in Swans Landing need help. Are we doing this or not?"

I looked at Sailor. She nodded. "I'll do it. To save Grandma and Swans Landing."

"I'll do it too," I said.

"So will I," Mara added.

"You sure?" I asked her. "You don't have to." Being human was the last bit of her mother she had left. I didn't want her to give that up.

"I'm sure," she told me. "It's my choice."

I nodded, then looked at Dylan. He had been quiet ever since we'd left the finfolk council.

Dylan closed his eyes, then shook his head.

"Why not?" Sailor asked sharply.

Dylan opened his clear blue eyes, his gaze focused on her. "I will help in the fight against Domnall. But I don't want to give up what little bit of human blood is in me. I just…can't."

"That's all you have to say?" Sailor asked. "We're trying to save our home and you *can't?*"

Dylan's jaw twitched, but he didn't break his focus on her gaze. "I don't want to be fully finfolk. I don't want to give up being human."

"Because of Elizabeth?" Sailor asked, her eyes narrowing.

"No," Dylan told her. "Because of me."

Sailor opened her mouth, but I held up my hand to her.

"It's okay," I told Dylan. "It's fine. We all have a choice here. No one has to do it. Any of you can back out now if you want."

I looked at Sailor and then Mara. But both remained silent.

Then I nodded and took a deep breath. "Okay then. Let's go talk to the council."

* * *

Pain seized my body. I bucked and thrashed, letting out a guttural scream. This was worse than changing between human and finfolk forms, worse than any pain I had ever felt in my life. My blood felt as if it were on fire, turning my bones into ash and cooking my organs.

I changed my mind. Leave me a mixture of human and finfolk. I couldn't survive this. My body was destroying itself from the inside out. How could I help Swans Landing if there was nothing of me left once this fire had burned its way through?

And then it was gone. The fire that seared through me was replaced by a cooling wave. I opened my eyes, blinking at my hands, which were still the same as they had always been. My silver scales gleamed in the algae light as I flicked my tail back and forth. Everything still worked. Everything felt whole and not burned to a crisp.

On either side of me, Mara and Sailor looked over their own bodies just as I had. They both appeared to be unharmed.

The finfolk gathered in the village square watched us with expectant faces. Dylan had been taken away from the square, so that the song wouldn't affect him as it had us.

"How do you feel?" Iomhar asked.

"The same as before," Sailor said. "It hurt, but now I don't feel any different."

Sorcha nodded. "The change is inside you. You will not notice any physical differences in yourself."

"So what you're saying is, losing the human part of us doesn't change who we are," Mara said, her eyes on me.

Finlay inclined his head. "That is correct. You no longer have the human weaknesses inside you, but otherwise you are the same."

"We are more than what we're made of," Mara said, smiling as she reached for my hand.

"So that's it?" I asked. "We can stand up to Domnall now and resist his song?"

"Aye," Iomhar said. "The song will not affect you the way it once did. We have done all we can do for you, if you insist on following through with this path."

"The offer to remain here still stands," Mairead said, gesturing toward the finfolk in the square. "You can return to your real home. You are part of us."

I looked at Mara and then Sailor. They both shook their heads.

"We have a home," I said. "But thank you."

We turned to follow the current out of the city, back to the door where Dylan would be waiting. As we started to swim away, Mara looked back and called, "Just so you know, being human isn't so bad either."

* * *

The blinding gold light faded and we were deposited back into murky, cold water that swirled around us. My hand was ripped from Mara's, but I didn't worry about losing her as I had before. Instead, I propelled myself toward the surface, certain that the others would do the same.

We surfaced a good distance off the beach, among frothy waves that battered us back and forth. I checked to make sure everyone was there—Mara wiping water from her eyes at my side, Dylan shaking his head some feet away, and Sailor bobbing on the waves behind him.

"Come on," I said, turning toward shore and diving back under to swim.

When my tail fin brushed the sandy bottom under the water, I broke the surface again. My body shed the scales and my tail became two legs as I made my way to shore. The beach was deserted and I inhaled sharply, afraid that Elizabeth had been discovered. But then a figure bounded from the darkness of the tree line, dark hair streaming on the wind behind her.

She wrapped her arms around Dylan's neck, hugging him tight. "You were gone for an eternity!" Elizabeth exclaimed. "I thought something had happened."

"We're fine," Dylan assured her. He closed his eyes as he hugged her to his chest.

When Elizabeth pulled back, she looked at the rest of us, her eyebrows raised. "So? Did you find it? Where are the rest of the finfolk?"

"They're not coming," I told her. "We're on our own."

Elizabeth's face crumpled. "They won't help us? What are we supposed to do?"

"They did help," Mara said. "They made us able to resist the song." She glanced at Dylan. "Well, most of us anyway."

Elizabeth shook her head. "I have no idea what you're talking about."

"Come on," I said. "We need to get moving. We'll explain on the way."

Chapter 27

"You need to keep a safe distance away," I told Dylan. "You and Elizabeth will be vulnerable to the song."

"I'm going with you," Elizabeth said, stepping forward. She glared at me, like she was daring me to contradict her.

But this wasn't a game and we didn't have time for her protests. "You're human," I pointed out. "You can be controlled as easily as the rest of them. You need to stay away."

Elizabeth crossed her arms. "And do what? Hide like a coward while you take these guys on? They have my daddy, Josh. I have to do something to help."

"Maybe we can," Dylan said, putting a hand on her arm. "We can go around and see who's left. Try to gather up some people to help us out if it comes down to a physical fight. There are still more of us than there are them. If you guys can keep the finfolk from singing, we can fight back."

"We'll do what we can," Mara told him. "Good luck getting people to join you. They didn't seem very eager to help us before."

Elizabeth tossed her hair back. "I'll *make* them listen."

"Be careful," Sailor told Dylan.

He nodded and then hugged her tight before reaching for Elizabeth's hand. The two of them ran off toward the homes where hopefully a few Swansers still remained who weren't under Domnall's control.

Mara, Sailor, and I walked down the abandoned Heron Avenue. We passed shops that had been closed for years and others that hadn't reopened in the last two days since the arrival of the Hether Blether finfolk. Dry leaves and crushed paper cups skittered across the asphalt around us. My wet hair dripped onto my hoodie, leaving a wet ring around my collar and I shivered in the cold breeze.

Something called me toward the beach. We crossed over the sand dunes, past the dry grass that waved back and forth in the wind, until the gray ocean opened up before us. Several yards away, a crowd of people stood on the golden sand. They didn't move toward us or away. They just stood there, watching as the three of us walked across the cold, wet sand.

As I drew closer, a sickening sensation washed over me. The crowd that waited for us wasn't only humans. There were finfolk too. Everyone that had gone out that morning to face Domnall were now under his control. Lake, Mr. and Mrs. Waverly, Mr. Moody, the other finfolk and humans I had grown up seeing on the island every day. They all stood together in a group, their eyes glassy and small smiles on their faces.

The song drifted on the wind toward us, but the gold bursts that always accompanied the notes didn't appear in my line of sight. I saw no visions from the song.

It had no effect on me now.

Domnall stood at the front of the group, his fists on his hips as he watched us approach. He narrowed his eyes and the song died.

"Something has changed about you," he said, looking the three of us up and down. He took a few steps across the sand, tilting his head. "You have been remade."

"Yes," I answered. "We've been to Finfolkaheem."

Behind him, the people still stood in a glassy-eyed trance, even though Domnall no longer sung. The song's effects sometimes took a while to shake off, especially after prolonged exposure. I didn't know how long we'd been in Finfolkaheem or how long the people here had been under Domnall's influence.

Domnall's eyes flashed at my words. "You appealed to the council for help, did you not? Where are they then?" He laughed as he turned a circle, his arms wide. "Where is your help from the great finfolk under the sea?" He dropped his hands and sneered at us. "They are not coming, are they? They have no concern for those of us above the surface. They closed the door on Hether Blether long ago, and they will do the same to you in the end."

"We don't need them," Mara said. "We'll fight you ourselves."

Domnall threw his head back and laughed. He waved at the people behind him. "And how will you do that, when I have your family and friends on my side?"

Some of the people shook their heads, as if clearing away fog from their minds. Domnall began to sing and once again, their faces took on that glassy, blank stare and soft smile.

"Where is Callum?" Sailor asked.

"Ah," Domnall said, grinning. "My dear brother-in-law. He is with us. Lochlan, bring him forward."

A guard dragged Callum to the front of the group. Or at least, I assumed it was Callum. He had the same red hair, but his face was swollen and bruised, his lip bleeding.

"Callum!" Sailor shouted. I had to grab her around the waist to keep her from running toward them.

Callum moaned, his eyelids fluttering.

"You bastard!" Sailor spat at Domnall.

"If he had not tried to kill me, I would not have had to do that," Domnall said. He shook his head. "Such a shame. He could have been a good king, I think, if he had not turned against his people and caused the death of his queen. His sister." Domnall's face twisted into a snarl. "My wife."

Lake shook his head, blinking as he looked around the beach. "What's going—"

And again, Domnall sang, erasing the thought from Lake's mind. Mara's body tensed next to me. I knew how she felt. I saw my mom in the crowd, the same blank look on her face. Despite what she had done and what I knew about her, part of me still wanted to protect her, as I always had.

How could we fight against this? Domnall had his guards, as well as a group of humans and finfolk he could control with his song. He knew about more about how the songs worked than I did. Whatever knowledge my ancestors had once had, we'd lost it over the past three hundred years. Even in my current form, I wasn't much more than an ordinary human.

There had to be another way. If we couldn't fight them physically, I had to use other methods of attack.

"Is that what this is all about?" I asked. "Revenge for your wife's death? So you take over a whole island just to make yourself feel better?"

Domnall glared at me. "Watch your tongue, young one. You do not want to press me."

"You're not the only one who has lost someone they love," I said. "My dad died before I even got to know him. Mara lost her mother. Sailor had lost hers until recently. Everyone here has lost someone we care about, but that doesn't give anyone the right to do what you're doing. Taking control of our people won't bring your wife back."

Domnall laughed. "Do you think I care about your people? Oh, yes, I told your sister I could take care of them and let them be true finfolk. But those were pretty words for a stupid girl to get her to tell me what I needed to know."

Sailor fought to break free of my grip, but I held tighter.

"No, young one," Domnall said, pacing back and forth across the shoreline. "What I really needed your island for was not the people, but what your people created here. When your people left Hether Blether, they did not realize that continuing the song in another place would create the same protection that hides the vanishing isles. Every time your people go to the water during the new moon, you have added another layer to the mists around your island. And with that, you have opened the door to the city under the sea. We cannot enter Finfolkaheem through Hether Blether any longer, but I can do so here with your island. All I need is peace enough to find the door, and the key you stole from me."

He looked at us. "Of course, now that you know where it is, I do not need to waste my time searching. You can tell me yourself."

I shook my head. "We won't tell you. You can kill us, but we won't talk."

Domnall's eyes flashed. "That can be arranged." He walked along the sand a few steps, then turned around to face us, his hands clasped behind his back. "Maybe we got off to the wrong start here. Maybe this violence and manipulation is unnecessary. We can be civil, can we not?"

At my side, Mara let out a snorting laugh. "Maybe some of us can."

"We both have things we want," Domnall said. "We could possibly reach an agreement that will benefit us both. You take me to the door to Finfolkaheem, and I will help you."

"What could we possibly want from you?" Sailor asked.

His gaze settled on her, staring hard. "Your mother is still ill, I presume? And I have found others that have suffered the same illness. I know what it is, and I know how you can heal her, heal *all* of them."

Sailor sucked in a deep breath. I could see the battle raging inside her. The thing she wanted most was to heal her mother and Miss Gale. I knew how she felt; I had wanted it for my own mother too, for as long I could remember. If Domnall was telling the truth, maybe that would happen.

He stepped toward us, his hand up in offering. "All you have to do is give me the key and take me to the door, and I will tell you everything you need to know."

"We can't trust him," Mara whispered, gripping Sailor's and my hands as we stepped back. "He's lying."

"I am a merciful person," Domnall said. "I only want what is best for all of us."

"No," Sailor said, her teeth clenched tight as she glared across the sand at him. "We won't help you."

I could see how much of an effort it was for her to turn down his offer. It stung me too, but we couldn't take any chances. We couldn't trust him.

"Very well." Domnall waved a hand at us. "Get them."

Artair and the other guards started across the sand toward us. I backed up, pushing Mara and Sailor behind me. My feet splashed in the surf as water lapped at the shore.

"You don't have to do this," I said, my gaze locked on Artair's face. I had seen his merciful side already. I needed to reach it again and convince him that Domnall was wrong.

But he didn't speak or acknowledge me. He continued forward, leading the other guards toward us.

My leg hit something hard and I almost toppled over. A slender boat sat on the sand, the end of it bobbing as the water rushed around it. The boat Domnall had arrived in. I scanned the bottom of the boat for weapons we could use, searching for an oar, but the boat was empty.

"Think of your daughter," I told Artair. "Would she want you to do this?"

"Aye, Artair," Domnall called behind him. "Think of your daughter. Precious little Iseabail. Think how you can help her, how finding the door will *help* her."

"What do we do?" Sailor asked, her hand gripping mine tight.

Mara bent down to grab a bottle partially buried in the sand and hurled it at the guards. Artair ducked, the bottle sailing harmlessly past him.

"Josh," Mara said, her voice cracking. "Ideas?"

"Only one," I muttered. It was an idea that my conscience fought against. I didn't even know if I could do it, but I had no other choice.

I began to sing, focusing my gaze on the crowd of humans and mixed human-finfolk behind Domnall. Mara and Sailor followed my lead, humming as loud as we could to fight Domnall's song.

The crowd, which had been standing behind Domnall, turned their faces toward us. They didn't look at us, their gazes were still unfocused and they saw only things they could see. But they followed the sound of our voices, moving toward us.

Could we make them attack Domnall? I didn't know exactly how to use the song, and my attempt at it now had only been a guess. Something twisted in my gut when I caught sight of my mother's vacant face in the crowd.

I couldn't make these people attack Domnall, even if I could figure out how. It was too dangerous to them. The only thing I could do was get them away from him. Maybe I could save them even if I couldn't save the three of us.

But Domnall fought back. He narrowed his eyes, his muscles tensed as he sang louder. The shuffling crowd stopped, their bodies trembling as they tried to decide who to follow. Mr. Moody fell to his knees in the sand, letting out a guttural growl. Others looked to be in pain, their minds torn between the two songs.

"Stop," I told Mara and Sailor. "We can't do this to them."

The finfolk guard closed in on us, Artair's expression blank and detached as he pointed the steak knife he still carried at my throat. I swallowed, gripping Mara and Sailor's hands tight. What had the finfolk council expected us to do on our own? Even changed, in this new fully finfolk form, we were no match for finfolk who knew how to use the song to their advantage.

It would end here. We had given up a part of ourselves for nothing.

A sudden roar filled the air, breaking my focus on Artair. My head whipped toward the dunes, where a crowd surged over the sand, fists raised, bats waving back and forth. I recognized Kyle McCutcheon from school and his friends, and Jackie and the other girls Elizabeth hung out with, and several other students from Swans Landing School, along with their parents and a few teachers. They all wore earmuffs and headphones, an obvious attempt to keep themselves from hearing the song.

Dylan and Elizabeth were at the front of the pack, racing across the beach toward us.

Chapter 28

Domnall's eyes widened when he saw the crowd racing across the beach. He opened his mouth and the first few notes of the song filled the air over the sound of the crashing waves.

The earmuffs and headphones didn't work very well at blocking out all sounds. Elizabeth faltered, stumbling a bit in her run across the sand. Then Dylan stopped running, his furious expression melting into nothingness.

"We have to keep Domnall from singing," I told Mara and Sailor. I lunged forward, pushing past Artair, who was still watching the crowd of humans. I fought my way through the finfolk guards and splashed back down the beach to where Domnall stood with the rest of the finfolk and humans he had already taken. His back was to me, his focus on the crowd near the dunes.

I crashed into Domnall, slamming my shoulder into his back. We tumbled to the ground, rolling across the sand. Domnall's song died as he struggled to push me off of him. He rolled me over, slamming my back into the wet sand and knocking the air out of me for a moment. My head spun as a wave rolled in, lapping at my side and soaking my sleeve.

"Get off of him!" Mara shoved Domnall, pushing him into the ankle deep water. She reached out a hand to help me back to my feet. My head still spun a little from the impact of hitting the hard wet earth and also the effects of the salt water that I now stood in. I felt it calling to me, wanting me to swim, the change already making me shudder deep inside.

"You have been an exceptionally bothersome little nuisance since the moment I met you," Domnall said, his furious glare directed at me. "I should have taken care of you before you had a chance to leave Hether Blether."

I backed away, pulling Mara with me. Domnall splashed through the water as he followed. The scar across his face stood out white against his red skin. He breathed heavily, his nostrils flared.

"What are you going to do?" Mara asked. "Kill us in front of all these people?"

"You will be only one of many casualties today," Domnall said, "unless you step aside and stay out of my way."

"You can't do anything to us," I told him. "You can't kill finfolk, you said so yourself."

"The laws be damned!" Domnall roared. "I am king and I answer to no one!"

My body trembled as the water soaked my jeans and lapped against my legs. The urge to dive in was almost too hard to resist. Mara shuddered at my side, her face pale and her teeth gritted together as she too fought against the change. We couldn't change now and leave everyone else behind. We had to stay, to find a way to fight back against Domnall.

Domnall's glare deepened as he drew closer. He was focused on us, as if he didn't even notice the cold water that crashed against his knees. His body was rigid, his teeth bared in a snarl. Another shudder rocked my body as I fought against the change that wanted to take over—

My eyes widened. *Domnall didn't notice the water.* At my side, Mara panted, her body shaking almost violently against the change. But Domnall stood tall and still. He didn't shudder like Mara and I did. He didn't look like he felt any pain as he fought to hold the change back.

Think, Josh, a voice in my head said. *You have all the pieces to the answer.*

Domnall's boat still bobbed along the shore farther down the beach, where the humans fought with the guards. He had always ridden in a boat whenever he crossed the water in Hether Blether.

He had come ashore in Swans Landing in a boat also.

My gaze focused on the scar etched across his face. A scar that could have been easily healed and erased for any finfolk by using the song.

It all clicked in my head as if someone had suddenly tapped me on the shoulder and whispered the answer in my ear.

"You can't change," I said out loud.

Domnall froze, his eyes widening. "What did you say?" he demanded, his teeth clenched.

"You can't change form," I repeated, my voice growing louder, confident that I knew the secret Domnall had been hiding. "You're not fully finfolk. Your family mixed with the humans that were brought to Hether Blether, didn't they?"

Domnall's face turned red and he lunged toward us, letting out a guttural scream.

Just before he reached us, another body crashed into him, pushing Domnall deeper into the water. The two figures emerged, splashing and struggling in the knee deep water. Lake's long hair whipped at his face as he fought against Domnall.

"Go!" he shouted at us before swinging at Domnall again.

Mara grabbed my hand and we crashed through the water toward the shore, where the rest of the humans and finfolk that had been under Domnall's spell were regaining consciousness.

* * *

"What the hell is going on?" Mr. Connors grabbed my arm as Mara and I crashed onto the beach. "What have you done, boy?"

"We've saved your life," Mara snapped. She shoved Mr. Connors back, forcing him to let go of me. "Now are you going to help us save this island or not?"

Mr. Connors looked back and forth between us, his lips curled in disgust. A scream echoed across the beach and his head whipped in that direction. "Lizzie!" he called, before taking off down the beach.

Lake and Domnall still struggled out in the water. Lake couldn't fight him on his own. If Domnall got the chance to sing again, he'd easily overpower Lake.

"Stay here," I told Mara.

She shook her head. "No way."

I gritted my teeth, then dashed into the surf, sending up splashes of water around me as I made my way back to Lake and Domnall. The finfolk king had gotten the upper hand and as I drew closer, I could hear him singing. Lake sat in the surf, the water crashing around his head. He had the glazed expression again and he lifted one hand to touch at something only he could see.

I leaped at Domnall, spinning him around. His song ended abruptly as we fell into the water again.

Domnall raised up on his knees, his hands pushing me underwater. I looked up at him through the rippling surface, his hair wet strings that dripped down his shoulders and his face contorted into a snarl. He seemed to remember that I wasn't like him. The water couldn't drown me.

He snatched me up by the collar, his hands moving to my neck.

"The laws of the finfolk do not protect you here," he told me. His thumbs dug into my windpipe, crushing against the

189

thin bones in my neck. I scratched at his hands, but his grip was strong. "I can kill you if I choose."

Lake crashed into Domnall again and all three of us tumbled into the water. Domnall came up, sputtering and coughing, shaking the water from his eyes.

"Get out of here," Lake told me.

But the change was taking over him. His body shuddered and he cried out, bending over at the waist as his legs began to morph into a tail, ripping through the fabric of his jeans. I could feel my own change aching deep inside, and I tried to force it back, hoping for just a few more minutes.

Lake disappeared under the water, leaving me alone with Domnall.

"Enough of these games," Domnall said. He reached into a pocket of his robe and pulled out a long metal object. Mr. Connors's handgun.

I swallowed, my eyes locked on the gun.

"Pathetic human weaponry," Domnall said, wrinkling his nose at the wet gun. "Crude, but effective enough, I suppose. I am certain I can figure out how it works."

He aimed the barrel at my chest, a smile curling the corners of his lips.

"No!"

A crack echoed across the water just as the dark shape of a figure leaped in front of me, pushing me back. I stumbled and fell into the surf, immersed completely in the water that bubbled in my ears and crashed over my head. I couldn't hold it back now. My body rocked with tendrils of pain as the change took over. I scrambled to unbutton my soaked jeans and tried to pull them off before my legs fused together. I tumbled backward, twisting in the relentless crashing waves that battered me back and forth.

When it was done and the pain subsided, I pushed myself toward the surface, blinking away the salt in my eyes, scanning the water around me.

Domnall stood in the surf, his wet robe twisted around his knees, the gun still gripped in one hand. He had a fiendish look, like a dog who'd had a taste of blood. He aimed the gun at me again, his teeth bared.

But before he could pull the trigger, a figure rose from the water behind him, golden scales flashing in the faint sunlight. Lake grabbed Domnall around the waist and pulled him into the water. Domnall's arms flailed, the gun soaring from his hand and landing in the crashing waves. Domnall and Lake disappeared below the surface.

"Josh!"

Mara stood only a few feet away, struggling with something in the water as she made her way back to the shore. I dove and swam toward her, resurfacing just behind her.

When I saw what Mara was pulling to shore, iciness spread through my body.

My mother lay limp in the water, her eyes fluttering and her face way too pale. A dark stain blossomed on the front of her shirt, turning the water around her red.

Mara and I pulled her to shore, getting her away from the rolling waves. The beach was quiet as people gathered around us, solemn faces looking down at my mom where she lay on the sand.

"Mom?" I asked, panting heavily. "Mom, talk to me. Open your eyes."

Her eyes fluttered a little and she let out a soft moan.

I looked up at the watching crowd. "We need a doctor!" I shouted at them. "Someone help!" But there was no hospital in Swans Landing. The closest one was a three hour ferry ride away.

Dr. Hansen knelt next to me, placing her fingertips on Mom's throat. Her mouth set in a grim line as she looked at me, the unspoken words evident in her eyes.

I spotted Artair in the group and pointed at him. "This is your fault. Do something!"

He came toward me, kneeling at my side. "What would you have me do?"

Tears burned my eyes and I blinked them back. "Sing. Heal her!"

Artair shook his head. "It does not work for humans."

"You have to try," I grunted at him.

"I am sorry," Artair said, lowering his head.

I choked on the lump in my throat. I bent over my mom, smoothing her hair back from her face. If he wouldn't try, I would. I began to hum the first notes of the song, stumbling over the sounds as I fought back sobs.

Mom opened her eyes, her gaze flitting back and forth until she focused on my face for just a moment. She smiled and reached up a hand toward me. She opened her mouth, but no words came out.

Her eyes closed slowly, fluttering for a moment, and then her hand fell back in the sand, unmoving.

Chapter 29

Mara's arms wrapped around me and I buried my face in her shoulder. She hugged me close, not saying anything, just sitting there with me. I couldn't look at my mom. She almost looked like she was sleeping, but I knew she would never wake up.

The numbness that had taken hold of me was now replaced by fury that sparked inside my gut. I wanted someone to blame, someone to lash out at.

I lifted my head and met Artair's gaze. He still knelt next to me, his mouth set in a straight line.

"Are you happy now?" I asked him. I slipped from Mara's embrace and stood, glaring down at the finfolk guard. "See what you did? Is this what you wanted, to come here and kill us?"

Artair didn't even look at me. "I never wanted anyone to be hurt," he said softly.

I laughed. "Well, that went according to plan, didn't it?" I had the urge to kick him, punch him, beat him until he could feel what I felt. I wanted him to hurt, to know what it was like to lose someone you couldn't save.

"I did not wish to come here," Artair said. "I was only following the orders of my king."

"Your king is dead," Lake said, stepping into the circle. His pants hung in tattered rags around his waist and he dripped water onto the sand. His face was scratched with deep lines, like he had been clawed. The left sleeve of his shirt gaped open and he pressed his hand to a gushing wound, red streams falling between his fingers.

Mara leaped to her feet, gasping. "What happened?"

Lake shrugged as he looked down at his arm. "Shark," he said simply. His eyes met Artair's. "Your king couldn't change. I took him out farther into the water to get him away from Josh. I expected him to swim and follow me back to shore. By the time I realized he wasn't changing, he had already gone below the surface and out of sight." He took a deep, shuddering breath. "The shark attacked me first. When I fought it off, it went after Domnall."

Artair and the other finfolk guards bowed their heads, all silent.

"So he wasn't finfolk after all?" Sailor asked.

"He was finfolk," Artair said. "But some of our people mixed with the humans that once lived among us in Hether Blether. Some finfolk still carry the human genes. Domnall was one of the unlucky ones, without the ability to change."

My gaze flickered to Callum, who still lay on the sand, his face bloodied and bruised. His eyes were closed, his breathing ragged. "Does Callum know?"

Artair shook his head. "Domnall was careful to keep everyone from knowing. Only I knew the truth. And our queen knew. She loved him despite his disability."

I ignored the comment about human genes being a disability. "What did he want with Finfolkaheem?" I asked. "Why did he come here?"

"He wanted the finfolk to do to him what they did for you," Artair said. "He wanted to be remade fully finfolk."

Silence fell over the beach. I turned my head, trying to keep from looking at the body of my mom still in the sand in front of me. Fury bubbled through me, but I felt tired, too exhausted to let it all out.

"What do we do now?" Dylan asked. He glared at Artair. "What do we do with them?"

"I say we do to them what they did to Silvia," Mr. Connors growled. He grinned cruelly as he looked at the finfolk guard. Some people agreed with his statement, nodding and clapping.

Mr. Moody scratched his chin. "Ain't none of you as affected by what happened as that boy there," he said, nodding at me. "So I say we let him decide. He's earned it, by my reckoning."

I looked at Artair, who gazed back at me without flinching. His face was lined and I could see the fatigue and sadness in his eyes. He would take whatever punishment I gave him, I knew.

But I just wanted the island back and I wanted everything to end.

"Heal Callum and Lake," I told him. "Then leave our island. Don't ever come back."

Artair inclined his head once. He motioned to the other guards and they followed him across the beach to where Callum lay. Everyone watched in silence as the guards carried Callum to the water. Lake followed behind until they were far enough offshore that we wouldn't hear them sing.

They did for Callum and Lake what couldn't be done for my mom. I stood on the shore, watching as the two men slipped below the water. They had done so much for me, this was just the smallest way I could repay them.

"Why are you doing this, boy?" Mr. Connors asked, his beady eyes flashing. "They killed your mama. These people killed both of your parents."

I shook my head. "My mom told me what happened the night my dad died and the finfolk didn't have anything to do with it. It was, as they've always said, an accident." There was no need to tell everyone what my mom had done. I wanted to let her memory rest in peace. "Only one finfolk killed my mother, and he's now dead too. We can't keep blaming each other. Don't you see that's what's caused all of our problems? We're *all* Swansers here. This island belongs to all of us." My shoulders dropped as energy drained out of me. "It's time to move on."

Mara gave me an encouraging smile as she stepped to my side, slipping her arm through mine. Sailor pushed past Mr. Connors and stepped up to my other side, entwining her fingers in mine. Dylan did the same with her other hand.

Elizabeth looked at her dad, biting her lip. Then she dashed across the sand to Dylan's side, leaning her head against his shoulder.

Mr. Moody hobbled across the sand. His eyes shone with unshed tears as he placed a hand on Sailor's shoulder, his beard curling as he smiled.

Others came too, finfolk and human. We formed a long line at the water's edge, watching the finfolk in the water.

* * *

Sailor threw her arms around Callum when he swam close to the shore. His face was red where the bruises had once been, but he seemed okay and he was awake again.

"Are you okay?" Sailor asked, checking him over.

He nodded. "I'm fine."

Sailor handed him the prosthetic she had found lying on the beach and Callum strapped it to his leg.

He looked back at the finfolk, who swam in the water behind him. Artair was the only one who made his way toward the shore, shedding his finfolk form as he rose from the water.

He bowed to Callum. "My king."

Callum's brow furrowed and he shook his head. "I am not your king. I was never meant to be."

Artair blinked. "We have no one to lead us now. We need a king."

"I'm sure you're capable of leading yourselves," Callum said. "You don't need me or anyone else."

Artair looked agitated as Callum started to walk away. "But it is the way we have always lived. The finfolk of Hether Blether need someone to guide them."

Callum looked over his shoulder and said, "Then you do it."

Artair stopped, his mouth dropping open. "I cannot…"

"You can do it just as well as I could," Callum said. "You're king now."

Mara raised her eyebrows. "That's it? You can pass off your title to someone else just like that?"

"Should I make a ceremony out of it?" Callum asked. He turned back to Artair, waved his hands around the man's head and then bent down, grabbed a handful of sand and rubbed it on Artair's cheeks. "By all powers born to me, I name you king of Hether Blether forever. There. Done. Good-bye, Artair."

Callum limped across the sand, Sailor at his side. A laugh bubbled out of me. I couldn't hold it back. Mara covered her mouth with her hand, but she couldn't hide her smile.

Artair wiped at the sand on his face, then turned toward me. He inclined his head, bowing slightly.

"I hope you will not think badly of us," he told me. "I am very sorry for the loss of your mother and for the pain we caused your people."

I shook my head. "I don't want your apologies. I just want you to go."

Artair nodded. "You have to understand that we all had our own hopes that would come from this journey. I followed the orders of my king, yes, but I also came to help my daughter." He swallowed, his expression pained. "Iseabail is…" He hesitated, taking a deep breath.

I thought of the time Sailor and I had seen Artair with his family at the beach. His wife had been in the water, swimming with their daughter. The finfolk woman had lifted the little girl out of the water and her feet kicked as she laughed above the waves.

"She's human," I finished.

Artair closed his eyes. "My wife's grandmother was human. Our daughter does not have the ability to change."

"So you wanted the same thing Domnall did," Mara said. "To have the finfolk remake her."

"I thought I did," Artair said. "I believed Domnall when he told me humans were weak, that they were killing our island." His gaze scanned over the crowd stretched out on the beach, human and finfolk. "But maybe we do not understand humans like we thought we did."

He bowed again and said, "You are welcome in Hether Blether any time you wish to come."

As I watched him disappear into the Atlantic, I said to myself, "I think I'll stay right here."

Chapter 30

Silence followed as I walked through every room of the house I had spent my life in. I had never taken much notice of the house. I knew it was falling apart, but it would never bother me much if I never looked too hard at it.

Now I looked. I saw the layers of dust that coated the bookshelves, full of books that no one ever read. I saw the chipped and cracked figurines that had been broken for as long as I could remember. I saw the couch with the rip in the armrest where the stuffing was falling out. The faded pictures on the walls. The cabinet doors that hung crooked on their hinges. The mildew that grew on the wall by the refrigerator because the appliance leaked.

I saw the cracked glass of the window in the front door. The carpet that hadn't been vacuumed in months. The dishes stacked in the sink.

I sat down on the couch, resting my head in my hands. The house had been decaying for a long time, probably even before my father died.

But there was some good here. Memories and ghosts haunted my mind. My mom in fleeting moments of clarity, picking me up for a hug or playing with me on the floor. We used to build sprawling cities I had never seen with a mix of old boxes, stacked books, and plastic blocks. She used to take me for walks around the neighborhood, up to the dock where we'd watch the people getting on and off the ferry and talk about all the places we'd visit one day.

And she would warn me to never go into the water. To stay as far from it as I could because there were things there that would hurt me.

I closed my eyes and began to hum, singing the notes I'd heard the finfolk sing many times from my hideout within the trees at Pirate's Cove. I had never joined them for song night, but I had learned the song through listening to it each month and could sing the notes as well as they did.

As the song filled the air within the room, I lifted my head and opened my eyes.

But there was nothing. The part of me that had been human wasn't there anymore. My mom and my dad were gone from me forever.

A knock at the door startled me and I let the song die. I sat on the couch, staring at the closed door. I could see a shape behind the curtain over the glass, but couldn't make out who it was. Mara had wanted to come with me, but I had told her I wanted a few minutes to myself. That was probably her now, coming over anyway to keep me company.

But when I opened the door, it wasn't Mara. It was her dad.

"Mr. Westray," I said, blinking. "What are you doing here?"

Lake ran a hand through his hair. "Please, Josh, call me Lake," he said. He stuffed his hands into the pockets of his cut off khakis. "Can I come in?"

I stepped back and Lake walked into the house, looking around the room. My face flushed at the state of decay in the house. We rarely had visitors.

"Can I get you something to drink?" I asked.

Lake shook his head. "No, thank you. I just wanted to talk to you."

I swallowed. His tone made a tendril of fear creep through me. "Is everything okay? Is Mara okay?"

"She's fine," Lake said. "This isn't about her. It's about you."

We sat down in the living room, me on the couch and Lake perched on the edge of a sagging armchair. He clasped his hands together, his elbows resting on his knees.

"I want you to know," he started, his eyes on the floor, "that I will be happy to do anything I can to help you if you need it. I don't have much, but you're one of us, both as a Swanser and finfolk. We won't let you starve or go homeless."

"Thanks," I said. "I think I'll be staying with Sailor for a while. She said she'll ask Miss Gale about it." I was eighteen, legally an adult. No one needed to look after me, but I wasn't eager to live in this house alone at the moment.

Lake nodded. "Good. You should be with family." He paused, dropping his gaze again. "I wanted to come apologize to you, Josh. For everything that's happened."

"You don't owe me an apology," I told him. "You didn't do anything."

But Lake twisted his hands around each other. "I feel like I'm somewhat responsible. I was friends with your dad. He used to come out on my boat with me to take notes about the fish population. He was always studying those fish. I think he knew more about what was coming than the rest of us could have ever guessed."

I smiled, imagining my dad out there on the water, recording all of the thoughts and theories that helped me save Swans Landing. He couldn't have known that I would use his notes one day, but I liked to think that maybe he was writing them down for me, for the future.

"The night your dad died," Lake went on, "we were supposed to meet to practice his singing. He was human, but he could sing like the rest of us. It was really amazing. He wanted to be out on the water that night, but I convinced him to stay far enough away that he wouldn't be able to hear the song too much, so maybe it wouldn't affect him like it would have if he was closer. We planned to meet at the pier as soon as I was done singing."

He sucked in a deep breath, holding it for a moment, then letting it out. "But when I got there, it was too late. I don't know, he must have fallen in. His body had already washed up on shore." Lake looked at me with shining eyes. "I'm sorry, Josh. I tried, but I couldn't save him."

I closed my eyes, not wanting to imagine my dad dead on the beach before I could even get to know him. My father's ghost and the things that might have been had haunted me thousands of times. Now they all crashed down on me as the truth about that night finally settled into my head.

I opened my eyes and looked back at Lake, who bit his lip, his hands clenched so tight his calloused fingers had turned white.

"It's not your fault," I said. "You don't owe me anything. You couldn't know what would happen that night and you didn't kill my dad."

"I feel like it's my fault," Lake said, his voice trembling a little. "If it hadn't been for me, maybe he wouldn't have been there."

Sucking in a deep breath, I said, "I know what happened that night. It wasn't you, it was my mom. She told me the truth. She pushed him in because she thought he was there waiting for Coral."

Lake's face crumpled and he buried his face in his hands for a long time. The room was silent, as was the world outside.

After a while, Lake lifted his head and looked at me with red-rimmed eyes. "I never suspected your mom had anything to do with it. She was a good woman, Josh. She needed help, but there was a part of her that was still good. She loved you a lot."

I didn't want to talk about my parents anymore. I stood and walked over to the kitchen, pulling a glass from a shelf. The water gurgled from the faucet as I filled the glass, shaking salt from the dirty shaker into the water.

"I need to go back to Finfolkaheem soon," I said, turning back to Lake. "We got rid of Domnall, but there's something else my dad wrote about. Another theory he had that I think explains the declining fish population and the crazy weather. And maybe even the strange illnesses people are suffering. I need to find out if there's a way to stop it."

Lake stood. "I'll go with you. I'll do whatever you need me to do."

I looked down at my glass, watching the water ripple across the surface. "You don't have to watch out for me, Lake. I'll be fine."

He walked over to me and put his hand on my shoulder. "I know, but I want to. Not just for your dad, but for Mara. She cares a lot about you." He smiled. "She has good taste. You're a great kid, Josh." He cleared his throat. "A great man."

I returned his smile. Maybe Lake Westray wasn't as bad of a father as everyone thought.

* * *

I shifted the backpack stuffed with clothes and a few other items from my house up higher on my shoulder as I turned the corner onto the street where the Moorings lived. Sailor had offered to share a room with her mom so that Callum and I could share the third bedroom. I figured that once Miss Gale was back on her feet, Callum would probably have to find a new place to live. Maybe we could be roommates. My mom's house had been paid for long ago with the money from my dad's life insurance. So we'd just have to pay for electricity and water, and food and other necessities. If we could both get jobs, maybe we could make it work.

It would be nice to have someone there with me, whenever I decided to go back home.

I had to think about positive things or else I'd see my mom dying all over again in my head. She would be buried in the Swans Landing cemetery next to my dad. She already had a plot, so that was taken care of. I just needed to plan the funeral, call the pastor at the church, order a casket, talk with a lawyer about getting everything she had changed to my name as her legal heir, and…probably a million other things I hadn't yet thought of.

A figure stood in the road just ahead, drawing me out of my thoughts. As I drew closer, I recognized Mr. Connors. He hadn't yet seen me, and he stood with his hands in his pockets, his gaze focused on the Mooring house.

"Can I help you?" I asked sharply.

He jumped, like I'd shocked him. The wind ruffled his dark hair and he narrowed his beady eyes at me. "Don't sneak up on people, boy," he said gruffly.

"What are you doing here?" I asked. "Aren't you done spying on finfolk yet?"

Mr. Connors's cheeks turned red just above his beard. "I ain't spying on nobody!"

"Could have fooled me," I said, crossing my arms. "You keep hanging around out here, watching the house but never knocking on the door. I'd call that suspicious behavior."

Mr. Connors sneered. "I guess you don't know everything after all, do you, boy?" Then he turned and stalked away, his head bent toward the ground. I pressed my lips together as I watched him walk away, until he turned a corner and was gone.

The house was warm and full of sound. Sailor and Callum sat on the couch, watching TV. Callum's arm was around Sailor's shoulders and she leaned into him. They looked over at me when I entered the front door.

"Grandma woke up earlier," Sailor told me. "I asked her about you staying here and she's fine with it."

I nodded. "Thanks." I set my bag down by the couch. "How is she doing?"

Sailor frowned. "Still sick, but getting better I think. I just don't know what's wrong with her."

"I have an idea," I said. "Domnall said that Hether Blether had experienced sickness and disease, which he believed was from the humans that had once been there."

Callum gave me a wary look. "You're not listening to things Domnall said, are you?"

I held up my hand. "Not just him. My dad wrote about what he thought was happening to Swans Landing and what he thought had happened before with Hildaland. If Swans Landing is changing, maybe Domnall was right in one way. The people are affected by the change too. Hether Blether's protection is fading, causing changes to the island and the people there. Our protection over Swans Landing is growing, causing those same changes here."

"So you think my grandma is sick because of the island?" Sailor asked.

"Maybe," I said. "She's not the only one. Look what happened to my mom. And your mom, maybe the change from Swans Landing to Hether Blether is what made her the way she is. Maybe other sicknesses here have been related to the changes the island is going through, but we just didn't know it."

Sailor sat up, giving me a skeptical look. "Okay, but what about us? We went from Swans Landing to Hether Blether and back, and we're not sick."

"We're younger," I pointed out. "That was also one of Domnall's theories, remember?"

Sailor made a face and settled back into the couch, next to Callum. "I don't want to think about Domnall. Not for the rest of my life."

Callum frowned. "I don't think I'll ever stop thinking about him."

"Did you know he was human?" I asked.

Callum shook his head. "No. He hid it very well."

"Are you sorry you're not going back to Hether Blether?" I asked.

Callum tilted his head to the side, then said, "No. I gave up my home four years ago. I have no claim there anymore." He looked at Sailor and smiled. "I think I can be happier here."

I resisted the urge to make a face at the two of them cuddling so close.

"I'm going to the bathroom," I said, heading toward the hall.

But I didn't go into the little bathroom. Instead, I walked past it to the room at the end of the hall. The door was open a little, but I knocked as I peeked in.

Coral sat at her desk, her hand moving across a paper as she shaded in lines. I stepped quietly across the room and gazed down at the picture. It was Pirate's Cove. I could recognize that little slip of beach anywhere. She drew three figures standing near the water: a girl with long blonde hair, a guy with shoulder length dark hair and wearing cut off khakis, and a guy dressed in jeans and a plaid shirt, a scruffy beard already beginning to show on his cheeks.

"Coral," I said as I sat on the edge of her bed. "Did you have an affair with my dad?"

She looked at me, blinking. She didn't answer.

I sighed and tried again. "Coral, did you—do you love Harry Connors?"

Her face dissolved into a frown. "He's getting married, but he doesn't love her. He loves me, he told me he does. He *still* loves me."

I felt cold and numb as a tingling sensation spread over my scalp and then down my back. All the pieces moved around in my head like a puzzle, falling into just the right spots, clicking into place so I could see the big picture.

"Who is Sailor's father?" I asked in a low voice.

Coral looked down at her lap, touching a hand gently to her stomach. "He'll love our baby, once he knows. He won't marry her. He can't marry her, he loves me." She looked up at me, her eyes wide. "Harry has *always* loved me."

I blinked quickly to keep back the tears that stung my eyes.

"You didn't have an affair with my dad, did you?" I asked. "It was Mr. Connors. He's Sailor's father."

But how had the truth gotten so mixed up?

"You never told anyone who Sailor's father was," I guessed. "You were spending so much time helping my dad that everyone just assumed."

Mr. Connors probably thought it was true too. Or maybe it was his easy way out rather than admitting to cheating on his fiancé.

"I wish Lake and Harry could be friends again," Coral said, turning back to her drawing. "The way it used to be." She picked up her pencil and began shading in the lines of the water as it lapped at the toes of the three figures on the beach. "I wish things didn't have to change."

"So do I," I told her.

Sailor and Callum were engaged in a playful fight over the remote control when I walked back down the hall. I stood in the shadows for a moment, studying Sailor as if I had never really looked at her. I didn't know why it hadn't dawned on me before now. She had never looked much like me, or even like my dad in the few pictures I had. She looked a lot like her mother, but there was something else there. The dark hair, the green eyes, the rounded nose.

She wasn't my sister. She was Elizabeth's.

But I knew I couldn't tell her that. Not right now, not after everything she'd already been through in her life. Elizabeth, even if she had changed her mind about finfolk, could never be the sibling Sailor needed.

I would be her brother for as long as she needed me to.

"Hey, you," Sailor said, spotting me loitering in the hall. "Tell Callum that it's my house, so I get to decide what we watch."

Callum groaned. "Please no. She's trying to make me watch one of those ridiculous American teen movies." He shot me a pleading look. "End the misery, please."

I walked into the room and threw myself onto the love seat. "Sorry," I told him. "Swansers stick together."

The truth was, I needed her just as much as she needed me.

Chapter 31

"You do realize the consequences of what you are asking?" Sorcha looked at me with wide, unblinking eyes.

I nodded. "We're not part of your world. We want to remain in the human world. We can't let Swans Landing vanish."

The four members of the finfolk council looked at each other, their faces solemn. I floated nearby with Mara, Dylan, Sailor, Callum, and Lake. We had come to ask the council how to break the mists that were covering Swans Landing and return the island permanently to the human world. I tried to block out the music in the water around me, but already I felt the tension inside me disappearing. The temptation to stay in Finfolkaheem nudged at my mind, but I fought to push it away. This wasn't my home, even if the human part of me was gone. I belonged in the world above the ocean's surface.

"We have not lost an island since Hildaland," Finlay said. "It is difficult for us to break the connection between Finfolkaheem and the vanishing isles. We are possessive and we do not like giving our property up so easily."

"With all due respect," Mara said, "Swans Landing does not belong just to the finfolk. The humans that live there have a right to it too."

"And these humans are your friends?" Mairead asked.

"Yes, they are," Dylan said.

"They're our family," I added.

Again, the council exchanged a look, like they were communicating without speaking. I didn't know if it was another thing the finfolk of the city under the sea were actually capable of or if they knew each other so well that it only seemed they could communicate through thought. There was so much about the finfolk that I didn't know. It made me think of my dad, and how he might have loved coming here to learn all of the finfolk history.

"The mists appeared because you sing the song of rebirth, the one tied to the water," Sorcha said at last. "It draws on the water in the air, turning it into the mists that hide the island. You can stop singing, which will cause the mists to weaken over time. It may take years before the effects are fully gone."

"There is a faster way, however," Mairead said. "You need to change the song and pull from the essence of the land. Tie the island back to the earth."

"Can you teach us the song?" Lake asked.

"You must wait until the new moon to try it," Iomhar said. "The start of the cycle of lunar rebirth will help you recreate your island. Sing during low tide, when you will be closer to the earth."

I nodded as I repeated the instructions to myself silently. New moon was still a few weeks away, so we'd have to wait before we could try it. Hopefully the island wouldn't fade anymore in the meantime.

The council taught us how to change the song we usually sang to pull from the earth's essence instead of the water. The earth songs were much more difficult to find and took more energy to use. That was probably the reason why we finfolk in Swans Landing had stopped using them long ago and forgotten them in favor of the easier water songs.

I didn't want all of this knowledge to be lost again once the door to Finfolkaheem closed off our shores. I would continue my dad's journals, I decided. Once I got back above the surface, I would write down everything I had learned in Finfolkaheem and everything I knew about Hether Blether.

"There's one more thing," Sailor said after we had all gotten the hang of the new song. "My grandmother. She's been sick for months. We think that the mists may be the cause. Is this true?"

"What are her symptoms?" Finlay asked.

"She's tired all the time," Sailor said. "She gets confused sometimes. A little fever, chills. It almost seems like a cold or flu, but it's lasted so long. And she's never been sick like this before." She glanced at me. "Others have been sick too. People who seem confused, my mother especially."

Sorcha inclined her head. "Do your grandmother and mother have human blood as well?"

"Yes," Sailor answered. "My grandmother's grandfather on her mother's side was human."

"The human blood is a weakness," Finlay said. When Sailor scowled and opened her mouth, he held up one hand. "I do not mean to offend you, but from the finfolk standpoint, it is a weakness. It allows illnesses, as you can see. The changes in the island affect the weakened human genes. Not only in mixed finfolk, but in humans themselves. They will all eventually succumb to the change."

Mara's eyes widened. "What do you mean succumb?"

Finlay's expression was grim. "If the changes on the island continue, they will not survive."

Miss Gale, Coral, Lake, Dylan, Elizabeth—everyone who still had mixed genes and all of the humans would die.

"What can we do?" I asked.

"Make sure they are with you when you sing to break the mists around the island," Sorcha said. "The song will affect everyone who hears it, and will renew and reconnect them to the human world as well."

Sailor nodded, smiling graciously at the council. "Thank you."

Iomhar gave us a sad smile. "When you sing the song, you will break the island's connection to Finfolkaheem. You will not be able to return. If any of you wish to stay, you may do so. But you must decide before the song is performed."

Callum nodded. "We can ask everyone above the surface who might want to come here, but..." He looked at the rest of us. "I think we've all made our decision."

"Yes, we have," I agreed. I was ready to get back home, even though this was probably the last time I'd see the city under the sea.

* * *

Cold rain battered the tent over the gravesite, dripping off the sides into the sandy grass below. I watched the rain fall, one drop after another.

The burial service had ended half an hour ago and everyone had drifted away, back to their dry homes. Almost everyone in Swans Landing had come. I had never before seen so many people at one funeral, human and finfolk both. Mom probably would have hated it, which made me laugh.

The silver casket I had ordered from the funeral home catalog still sat above ground. The men who did the job of lowering the casket and filling in the sand sat in their trucks on the other side of the graveyard, waiting for me to leave so they could do their job.

But I wasn't ready to go just yet. Once I walked away, that would be it. Both of my parents would lay in the ground and I'd be on my own, for the rest of my life.

Someone sat down next to me and slipped an arm through mine, leaning her head on my shoulder. Mara didn't say anything, she just sat there with me. I had seen the tears in her own eyes earlier and I knew this was hard for her, probably bringing up the memories of her own mother's funeral earlier that year.

Then Sailor arrived, sitting down on my other side. Callum joined her. The crunch of broken shells and sand behind me told me someone else was coming, and I looked over my shoulder to see Dylan and Elizabeth walking hand-in-hand toward us. Elizabeth wrapped her arms around my neck, hugging me tight, while Dylan put a hand on my shoulder.

We stayed there, just the six of us, for a long time. No one spoke, but I knew what they all meant.

None of us were alone.

Chapter 32

Three weeks later, I bounded down the steps from Mara's house. This was the first time I'd felt something close to normal since my mom's funeral. Mara and I had just gone out for lunch at one of the few places currently open in Swans Landing and I was on my way to go talk to Mr. Jasper at the Sand Dollar to see if maybe I could grovel and apologize enough to get my job back.

We were all trying to get back to normal around the island. It was hard, since the mists were still hanging around, thick and unrelenting. But soon it would be Song Night, and hopefully we could break the tie to Finfolkaheem and put the island back where it belonged in the human world. Then the ferry would come again and maybe even tourists with it.

"Josh."

I jumped at the voice behind me. I hadn't seen Dylan when I passed his house, so he must have come out and followed me.

"Hey," I said. "I'm going over to the Sand Dollar to see if I can get my old job back. Want to come?"

Dylan shifted from side to side. "No, um, thanks. I, uh, need to ask you for a favor."

He looked solemn, and I had a feeling this was a serious favor he was asking. Dylan and I had spent more time together over the last few weeks and were becoming somewhat friends, but it was still a bit strange for him to come to me for favors.

"Okay," I said. "Sure. What do you need?"

Dylan took a deep breath. "I need to go to Finfolkaheem. And I need you to go with me."

I blinked at him. "You want to go back? You're not…planning to stay there?"

We had met with the finfolk in Swans Landing and told them about the door to the city under the sea. We gave them the chance to go there permanently, to anyone interested in leaving the island. But no one had taken the offer so far.

"No," Dylan said. "There's something I want to do, and I have to go there in order to do it. But I need help." He shrugged. "I can't ask Sailor or Mara to do this. They would try to talk me out of it."

My skin prickled at the look on his face. "How do you know I won't try to talk you out of it?"

"I figured I could turn you down easier than I could either of them." He sighed again. "Will you take me there?"

"What is it you want to do?" I asked.

Dylan closed his eyes and said, "I want to be remade. To be human."

My mouth dropped open. I had never imagined a finfolk willingly giving up the ability to be finfolk. The ability to change was taken away from Callum without his choice and it must have been agony to not be a part of the water like he had once been.

"Do you know what that would mean?" I asked him. "You'd never be able to swim like we do. You'd be completely vulnerable to the effects of the song. You would never change form again."

"I know," Dylan said.

215

"You've spent your life being finfolk and connected to the water. You wouldn't have that anymore. A part of you would be gone."

Dylan stared back at me evenly. "You gave up part of yourself to help the island. I want to give up part of myself in order to live the life I want. It's *my* choice, Josh."

I glanced back at the house where Dylan lived with his family. "Do your parents know?"

"I talked with them about it last night," Dylan said. "They're not exactly thrilled, but they've given me the freedom to decide for myself what kind of life I want."

I thought about Mara and Sailor and how they'd react when they found out about this. They would probably kill me for taking Dylan to Finfolkaheem.

But he was right. It was his choice.

"Are you doing this for Elizabeth?" I asked. "You don't have to be human just to be with her."

Dylan shot me an annoyed scowl. "I'm not doing it for her. It's for me. Do you know what I see when I hear the song? I see myself, walking. Just walking as far as I want to go. Never swimming, never changing form. I've tried to be happy here. When Mara first arrived, I thought that maybe if I could love her, I could convince myself to be fine with my life as it is. But even if she had chosen me instead of you, I don't think it would have changed anything. I've thought about this for the last few months. It's not a spur of the moment thing. I know what I'm giving up, and I know what I'll gain. I'm ready."

My shoulders slumped, but I nodded. He sounded confident. It wasn't my choice to make. "Okay. Let's go."

As we walked toward Pirate's Cove, I kept waiting for Dylan to change his mind. As we stripped out of our clothes on the empty beach and waded into the water, I expected him to stay behind and say it was just a joke. As we crossed through the door to Finfolkaheem, I looked to see if there was any hesitation on his face. There was nothing except stern determination. Dylan swam confidently to the square where we found the council with many other finfolk.

The council listened to Dylan's request, their expressions blank and their mouths set in thin lines. I swam just behind him, waiting for them to tell him it was impossible. Or else that they wouldn't do it. There had to be some sort of ancient finfolk law about doing something like this.

But after exchanging a few looks, Mairead nodded and said, "We will grant your request, young one, if it is truly what you wish."

"It is," Dylan said.

Finlay looked at me. "You have already been changed, so the song will not affect you if you hear it. But you are necessary in this. Once the song is complete, his lungs will be the last part of him to change. You must get him back to the door and to the surface in your world, or else he will be capable of drowning, just as any other human."

I gulped. "I understand."

But I didn't really. I didn't understand why Dylan would do this. Taking away the finfolk part of him wouldn't save Swans Landing or anyone else. No one was asking him to do this. I looked at his tail of shimmering blue scales, knowing this was the last time anyone would see them.

I used to envy Dylan, back before everyone knew that I was finfolk. He had always seemed so sure of himself and who he was. He didn't apologize for being finfolk. He seemed comfortable in his own skin.

It was strange how sometimes you didn't really know a person the way you thought you did.

"Are you sure?" I asked Dylan, raising my eyebrows. "*Really* sure?"

He swished his tail back and forth through the water, looking down at it. Then he nodded. "I'm sure."

I didn't want to watch the transformation. I didn't want to see part of Dylan being taken away from him. I closed my eyes as the council began the song. Thousands of finfolk voices joined in around us, a haunting melody that sounded almost like a funeral song. It was a death in a way, but I hoped that it would give Dylan the life he wanted.

I opened my eyes as the song began to fade. Dylan no longer had the blue-scaled tail. His legs were two limbs again, his skin shining pale in the glowing algae around us. Pain contorted his face and he looked like he was going to be sick.

"Go," Sorcha told me. "Hurry."

I grabbed Dylan's arm and pulled him with me, pumping my tail fin as fast as I could to rocket through the water. He was mostly deadweight, barely moving his legs to help propel us.

The glow of the door appeared behind the rocks just ahead. I swam harder, biting my lip as we pushed through the water. Dylan began to struggle, flailing his arms and shaking his head.

Just a little more. I pushed Dylan through the door ahead of me. The whirlpool on the other side almost ripped him from my grasp, but I tightened my hold on his arm.

I fought against the current, pushing us toward the surface and out of the swirling water. Dylan came up next to me, sputtering and coughing.

I helped him swim to shore and then I shed my finfolk form as I walked back onto the beach. Dylan collapsed on the sand, panting heavily. I pulled my jeans on, shivering in the cold breeze, and then sat down next to him. The water crashed against the shore, just barely brushing Dylan's toes.

Toes he would have every day for the rest of his life.

"How do you feel?" I asked after a moment.

Dylan lifted his head, his cheek coated with a layer of sand. He smiled.

"I feel human," he said.

Chapter 33

Night fell and almost total darkness covered Swans Landing. Every finfolk on the island gathered on the beach at Pirate's Cove, our breaths hanging in the night air for a moment before dissolving into the mists.

The constant strobe of the lighthouse at the other end of the island was barely visible through the fog. It was getting thicker. Phone lines had gone dead a week ago. We didn't even know if the island existed in the human world at all anymore.

Tonight we'd find out if we could bring it back for good.

Mr. Moody sat on the beach with Miss Gale, her head in his lap. She was too tired to swim, so she would sit and listen to the rest of us sing. Coral sat next to them, humming to herself as she trailed her fingers through the sand. Other people—finfolk and human—all affected by the mists, sat along the beach, waiting.

"You sure you don't want to go back home and wait?" Callum asked Mr. Moody. "We don't know what this song might do to you or cause you to see."

But Mr. Moody shook his head. "I'm staying here, boy." He waved a hand toward the water. "Y'all go on and get it over with."

Sailor knelt to kiss her grandmother's forehead. "I'll come right back to you, Grandma. You'll feel better soon."

She stood and squeezed her mother's hand, then followed Callum to the water.

I saw Dylan's parents and his little brother as they made their way to the water. Dylan wasn't there. He had seemed to be happy with his decision to become human, and he and Elizabeth were talking about applying to colleges near each other in the fall.

If things had gone according to plan, if I had been just another human guy, I would be going off to college this summer. But my life had never been normal, from the moment I was born I was something else. Now I was something even more different than that, my human genes changed by the finfolk song.

"You ready?" Mara asked, giving me a smile.

We were always tied to the island, but it didn't have to limit my life. I would go back to school, get my GED through online classes. Maybe I could find an online oceanography or marine biology course. Something related to the water. Something that would have made my dad proud.

I nodded. "I'm ready."

Lake stood nearby, watching me with narrowed eyes. I let out a shaky breath. He *definitely* knew I had almost slept with his daughter. I was becoming used to his watching, silent presence, but still, I made sure not to look Mara's way as she shimmied out of her jeans, no matter how much I wanted to.

When we were all in the water and had changed forms, we turned to look back at the shore. We fell silent, listening to the crash of the waves around us and the hum of the earth below the water.

Then our voices filled the night, rising higher and louder into the mists all around us. The vibrations of both water and earth filled me. It would have been easy to become distracted by the loud water song that my body was so used to. But I closed my eyes, focusing all of my thoughts the softer, older earth song, pulling it through me and singing the notes that matched it.

We sang until my throat felt raw and my voice became hoarse. When the song finally ended, I almost felt like I had no energy left. It had taken a lot of power to pull from the earth's essence.

But the water around me had stilled. It no longer crashed and swirled as it had done ever since I'd arrived back in Swans Landing a month ago. When I opened my eyes, the night looked clearer. There was still no moon and very little light, but stars pinpricked the sky. In the east, the first orange tint of the sunrise was touching the horizon.

"Did we do it?" Mara asked, looking around us. Finfolk floated along the calm water, all of them looking for a sign that everything was okay.

"I think so," I said. The earth felt different, even the water felt different. The door to Finfolkaheem was closed and Swans Landing was back where it belonged in the human world.

We made our way back to the shore. Sailor pushed past me, hurrying over to her grandparents.

"Grandma?" she asked, kneeling in the sand. "Are you all right?"

Miss Gale's eyes stayed closed and she let out a soft moan.

"Gale?" Mr. Moody asked, leaning over her. "Say something. Let us know you're okay."

Miss Gale opened one eye and looked up at his grizzled face. She licked her cracked lips, then said in a voice that sounded more like the woman I'd always known, "I want a wedding. A real one. Right here. With a ridiculous wedding cake covered in flowers. Lemon cream in the middle." She pointed up at Mr. Moody. "And you don't you start in about how you hate lemon. You know you always eat my lemon pie when you think nobody's looking, so don't give me none of that. And you're moving to my house. There ain't no way we can live in that shack you own. There ain't even enough room for our girls over there."

Mr. Moody's mouth hung open a moment. Then he laughed and leaned forward, kissing Miss Gale on the lips.

Mara slipped her arm around me and grinned. "I guess it's a good night for a proposal," she said.

I laughed. "You want one too?"

She tilted her head to the side, tapping her finger on her chin. "Maybe in a few years. Once I decide whether I want to keep you or not."

"I knew you were just using me for my singing abilities," I said, sighing dramatically.

Mara laughed and then wrapped her arms around my neck, leaning her head back to look up at me. "I decided to keep you months ago."

I leaned down and kissed her, sending tingling sensations throughout me. If we had been alone, my hands wouldn't have been able to stay still.

I pulled back and caught sight of Lake watching us, his arms crossed. Oh, he knew. He definitely knew.

I was in *so* much trouble.

From the Author

Thank you all so much for your support of the *Swans Landing* series! These books were a work of love inspired by a trip to North Carolina's Outer Banks years ago. I wondered what kind of secrets the year-long residents might know about the islands that the rest of us don't get to see, and out of that came the idea for the story of the Swans Landing finfolk.

You can find stories about finfolk mythology online, but a lot of the information in these books is my own, created specifically for this story. Hildaland, Hether Blether, and Finfolkaheem are all taken from the finfolk mythology, but the details about them and what they look like came from my own imagination. If you want to read more about finfolk, I highly recommend the website Orkneyjar – The Heritage of the Orkney Islands: http://www.orkneyjar.com/.

You can also read more about Swans Landing and see the playlists I created for each book at www.shananorris.com.

About the Author

Most days, Shana Norris still feels like she's stuck at sixteen, which is probably why she enjoys writing about teens. She always wanted to be a mermaid and fell in love with the Outer Banks during a gray late winter years ago. She lives in a small town in eastern North Carolina with her husband and small zoo of pets, which currently includes two dogs, five cats, and five chickens.

To learn more about Swans Landing and the people living there, please visit www.shananorris.com.

Other books by Shana Norris:
The Boyfriend Thief
Troy High
Surfacing (Swans Landing Book 1)
Submerging (Swans Landing Book 2)
Shifting (Swans Landing Book 3)
Something to Blog About
The Secrets of You and Me